A DEATH
IN THE FAMILY

by the same author

DEEP DIVING

A DEATH
IN THE FAMILY

❦❦❦❦❦

Stephanie Conybeare

COLLINS
8 Grafton Street, London W1
1989

William Collins Sons & Co. Ltd
London · Glasgow · Sydney · Auckland
Toronto · Johannesburg

First published by Collins 1989

BRITISH LIBRARY CATALOGUING IN PUBLICATION DATA

Conybeare, Stephanie
A death in the family.
I. Title.
823'.914 [F]
ISBN 0-00-223535-8

Set in Linotron Galliard by
Rowland Phototypesetting Ltd
Bury St Edmunds, Suffolk
Printed and bound in Great Britain by
William Collins Sons & Co. Ltd, Glasgow

FOR ZOSIA AND JERZY
WITH FONDEST LOVE

For it is we who haunt the dead
And not the dead haunt us – even
We tempt them, if their love constrains them
Still to will what we desire.

ANNE RIDLER

ONE

❧❧❧❧❧❧❧❧❧❧❧❧❧❧❧❧❧

Mother died two weeks before I left Montana to spend Christmas with my niece, Nicola, in London. A telegram arrived from Dar es Salaam. Though I knew at once it must be to do with Mother, I was taken by surprise, shaken, shocked before I read it. We had not communicated for over forty years since I left home at the age of sixteen, so why now? What now? Slowed by agitation, a pain in the region of the heart, I brushed away the snow and read a tropical message of demise and condolence. Not from Mother but from her solicitor. An Indian, it would seem; Indian English. My lips curled in disdain at the lush Hindu sentiments obvious even in telegraphic shorthand – these people never change, I thought, no dignity, no tact, they never held a candle to Somalis. At first this was my only reaction; contempt and indignation that a total stranger, and such a one, should take it unto himself to tell me that Mother had died. How dare you! I said it aloud, the dogs leapt clear of me. Then I crumpled the telegram into a tight damp wad and dropped it into my kitchen wastepaper basket where it vanished from view along with other bits of unsolicited mail.

Mother had been dead to me for so many years that her physical conclusion meant nothing, and news of it was an unpardonable intrusion on my privacy. Who was to blame? Maybe Nicola. She was my only link with the past and she had kept in close touch with Mother – probably given her my address. But I could not blame Nicola, for anything. So instead, by default, personal guilt began to hurt my mind though I struggled to suppress its bitter message of reproach.

9

She died alone, it said, she died without you there; parents do not die properly without their children present. Which was rubbish, of course, like the superstitious nonsense Kikuyu servants used to talk. I reacted at once: not my fault in the least. I always quash self-criticism, never grant it time to fester. And yet when my voice broke surface again and I was talking to myself (as I often do, and why shouldn't I? I live alone) there was something in my tone which called the dogs back in a rush of canine concern, all tails and warm tongues, and I murmured, my darlings, I love you so much.

Then I went through the day as if nothing had happened. The news and the telegram simply would not exist; I did not have to try to forget them.

I made myself presentable (I have always believed in the importance of maintaining standards though nobody else seems to these days) and then drove to the supermarket through a blizzard with Shelley, the golden labrador, on the back seat. I miss her now – she was marvellous company, was old Shelley, with her big brown eyes and moist nose constantly seeking affectionate contact, and she was protection. Montana is no longer the quiet backwater it used to be thirty-five years ago; like my birthplace Kenya it was when I first came, all those open spaces and the personal freedom. But it has changed (as has East Africa for that matter) so that foreigners such as myself are less valued and less safe. In the old days I used to have food delivered to the house, then out of town, and grocers in Billings were only too glad to do it properly, but in recent years I found I could no longer trust the shops to send me decent goods or honest delivery boys who mightn't pull a knife or gun. So I bought a station wagon with an automatic locking system and took to driving to the supermarket – all of which seems a long time ago now, and exotic, as Husseini shops for me these days, carrying my *kikapu* on his bicycle into Kariakoo market.

*

Geographically my life has gone full circle. I am back in East Africa, back home, so to speak, though still a foreigner and always will be. Not that 'always' is such a long time in my case: my health being what it is a few more years are all I am vouchsafed, which is why the time has come to write – I must do it while I am able.

Two years have passed since the events which I am about to record and yet it is only now – now that an end is in sight, my end – that I can hold myself to the task of description and analysis. I do have answers, but they float; the time has come to fix them down on paper. Hold them still for posterity. I have always worked things out by scribbling in the firm belief that only the written word is real and reliable. Simple problems – such as where to leave the dogs at Christmas – these I set out in pros and cons, list possible solutions, summarize and conclude. I do it all on paper; without notes I should be lost.

Prose I reserve for higher things and deeper issues, and this piece of prose will locate me. It will clarify all; not just what I know already, but the things I shall discover as I go. Little details missed, subtle nuances.

I shall write in my voice of that time to let delusion speak its own truths. I had another voice then – younger, more cruel, livelier. I was more alive; I had not yet crossed that grey threshold beyond which the proximity of death becomes familiar, commonplace, and a matter of indifference. Of course, when I have finished writing my voice will have changed yet again.

I have always written. Mother saw to that. She started me dashing off diaries and it became a compulsion, a daily activity I could not do without, and the volumes of my life collected into a huge burgeoning mass of paper as if I carried my existence about with me like a shell which afforded no protection yet could not be shed. Though I did shed it in the end – I left all my notebooks behind in Montana.

Writing as I am, without references, without diaries to clutch for confirmation, I feel it is important to fix this time, my present, as a point of reference. Like taking bearings, or marking the entrance to a labyrinth. For some while, no doubt, I shall refer back to now and keep returning to it until I have gone too far. And the past has taken over, and I am there completely, among the events which followed Mother's death.

I remember that after I returned from the supermarket in Billings on the day the telegram arrived I did what I always did: unpacked, washed the kitchen floor clean of bits of snow and mud tracked in by Shelley, then fed her and the rest of the dogs. Come to Mother, I called, come, my beauties, just look at you. And I opened my arms to Byron, the border collie, who leapt up to be held, a feat of agility none of the others was clever enough to follow. Afterwards I made a cup of coffee for myself and sat down to write – poetry it would have been, as I always did my diary before breakfast. The dogs were wisely at my feet, I was concentrating well, when a muffled noise at the front door disturbed me. Disturbed the dogs; they ran and flung themselves against the door barking loudly.

This intrusion turned out to be a note from my neighbour, Muriel, who lives in a bungalow built ten years ago when the town began to move out to us. She was complaining about the dogs, yet again, and complaining by letter, moreover, without the courtesy of a knock on the door and face-to-face explanation. I was furious. Suddenly and instantaneously demented, I stood in the hallway overwhelmed with rage.

It is a kind of dislocation, anger, I find; a losing touch like fainting – the same dreadful sense of isolation despite the fact that anger is meant to include its object. Angry, one is aware of no one but oneself as the pressure of it builds towards a shattering crescendo. Physical pain, I understand, is rather the same – or so Nicola told me.

I acted swiftly and mechanically. I pulled on a coat and

boots and went round right away to confront Muriel with her stupidity and cowardice. I caught her by surprise, she was just taking off her outdoor clothing, and flung at her the full force of my indignation. How dare she object to my dogs! What did it matter if they dug in her garden, it was covered with snow, for God's sake. Such ridiculous idiocy, and to write a note, one simply does not behave that way. I can imagine how I looked to her: I towered over her, tall and straight, head back, hair strict, eyes fierce and unavoidable. Circling my wrath, like cold air about a fire, was absolute contempt. Muriel cowered like a reprimanded housemaid. She tried to say something like, 'Mrs Tollefson, just 'cause you're English don't mean . . .' Then she fled towards her kitchen. I hurled my last words after her: 'How dare you!'

Those words were unfortunate because, even before I was home again, they recalled the circumstances under which I had uttered them earlier that day. By the time I entered the house I felt as though I were suddenly thawing after hours of numbness, and the pain of it was like the pain of heat on frostbite. Blood rushed to my memory. I scrabbled for the crumpled telegram and found it, a tiny part of me. Too late: nothing now that I could ever do about Mother and me, about the way we were; not now that she was dead.

The typed words were gone, dissolved in snow and spite, nothing left, no softening Hindu platitudes to pretend consolation and forgiveness for the fact that she had died alone.

I felt condemned, imprisoned. Indeed, emotions heightened, it seemed to me that we were both damned by the absence of reconciliation: Mother might be dead but her spirit would never be released without my love, nor mine, when I died, without hers. The first love, that primary attachment; all I possessed of it was hatred, I had hated Mother as ardently as I might have loved her since early childhood. I never asked to be her child, nor did she invite me.

How dare you! This was aimed at Mother; nothing to do with her offending solicitor. How dare she die without me, without waiting for me, how could she? It was her final act of maternal malpractice to die without loving me, without letting me love her. I was frozen in my past for ever, no chance of reparation, I could only regret what never was. I felt as if a limb of mine had remained a foetal bud, and I had always expected it to grow, knew it could and would; yet suddenly, the means of its development was gone, like a blood supply cut off, and the little that was there would presently wither. I am talking about my ability to love anyone.

The sense of potential withheld, abolished, made me aware of my age. I had always felt young, yet the end of middle age was chronologically upon me, my sixtieth birthday being a few months away. Was there not a point at which people die before they die, a turning point when the body stops restoring itself incessantly, as if suffering a sudden loss of somatic optimism? Perhaps, but the mind was different, or mine was: I was suffering, pessimistic, but undefeated because there was a part of me, inherited from Mother, which would never give up, which would keep on trying and insisting when all means of doing so were gone.

I was kept busy for the next two weeks preparing for my departure to London. Or rather preparing Susan, my daughter, who was making the journey as well. Incapable of organizing the simplest domestic detail, she was totally at sea with such matters as how to send the boys to Denver to their father (who had divorced Susan two years earlier), what to tell her employers at the café where she worked, even how to lock up her caravan. Every day I drove from Billings to Big Timber where she lived, in what proved to be an ever increasing and frustrated struggle to make sure that my investment in her plane ticket would not be wasted. Unfortunately we were not flying together; I had booked too late for that. I would have to trust to fate and the small amount of sense Susan might still possess that she actually got from the Greyhound bus onto the right plane in Chicago.

Christmas in London had been my idea. A notion which came upon me very suddenly and insistently at the end of October, like something of grave importance forgotten and then fortuitously recalled. It seemed at the time as if I had always intended such a family gathering, when in fact the plan was entirely new, and I felt quite desperate about it, unstoppable, the way I always am when I want something badly even if, and especially when, there seems no logical reason for having it. I had to go, and felt that Susan had to come too. I said to myself, it must be this Christmas; if we are to have a family gathering it must be now or never.

I phoned Nicola long distance to suggest it. 'Darling, I know it's perfectly frightful of me to invite myself at the last moment – typical, isn't it? – but I only felt we really must have at least one Christmas together. I've never believed in planning years in advance – who knows where we'll all be next year at this time? In the grave most likely – Susan from drink, me from running these blasted dogs – my God, how the darlings have been tiring me out, tramping the hills like a trooper just so they can burrow after rabbits.'

A wispy voice at the other end: 'Oh, super, I . . . how good of you to come . . . marvellous, Augustus will be thrilled, and . . .' The voice trailed off into static and I remembered that Nicola never finished her sentences.

Augustus, I thought to myself afterwards: yes, and then there's Augustus, the doctor, who might well be of help with Susan.

In the back of my mind, too far back to be clear, was a sense of things somehow falling into place, happening correctly. Meant to happen. I was pleased and expectant about the plans I had made, and excited in nervous, agitated flashes of presentiment. I was doing what I always did: looking forward to things too much.

When the news came of Mother's death it seemed to take over all the arrangements, to absorb them, as if I had planned Christmas sensing the proximity of her demise. But why Mother's dying should send me to Nicola I had no idea, I could see no connection whatsoever. Nonetheless there was one, for when I was not thinking about Mother – who had repossessed my mind, who haunted me constantly since the telegram arrived – I was preoccupied with Nicola in an urgent, yearning fashion as though only she might restore calm and forgetfulness. I felt frantic to be with her, I needed her immediately, I had to have her by me. Yet I did not think I needed consoling, it was nothing like that, the conventional family situation of bereavement. It was more that I felt too full of Mother yet empty of the essence of her; cheated of the parts I required most, which ought to have been mine yet never were. I needed to talk about Mother and to have her spoken of by someone who loved her. To the best of my knowledge there was only one such someone: my niece Nicola.

TWO

❧❧❧❧❧❧❧❧❧❧❧❧❧❧❧❧❧❧

Airplane travel ought to be an opportunity to be nowhere, to relax the mind, to free the spirit of all earthly burdens. Yet my flight to London was devoid of such enlightenment: my mind turned obsessive as it tends to do easily – a nasty trick of neural chemistry that tormenting thoughts will replay and amplify incessantly, no matter how hard I struggle to suppress the insane repetition of what troubles me.

It was Mother I thought about and, in particular, one scene from my childhood which kept coming back to me again and again the way bad dreams do, recurring in slightly different versions until the dreamer wakes. This scene was significant, I thought, for hidden meanings, the yearnings it concealed. What was said was flotsam, superficial, the dialogue not dialogue but desultory, disconnected speeches, because it was unspoken words beneath the surface which communicated. Until the end. Odd really, the way tension can create a sound of aimlessness with catastrophe so close at hand.

Although this particular scene by no means commenced bad relations between Mother and myself, it nonetheless encapsulated, demonstrated, all that was wrong. And the main event of lasting consequence was a formal declaration of the absence of love; this was for me the official beginning of our estrangement.

It happened when we lived at Naivasha. On my sixth birthday. A long time ago, yes, but a six-year-old's perception and recording memory are crystal clear, in perfect order, their eyes and instincts keen and undistracted. Prejudice occurs later through adult selectivity – selecting what we wish to remember – not in the childhood images themselves. I was only six but still, even today, I see this particular sequence as if it were yesterday. Because of its significance.

We are having breakfast on the verandah, Mother, my father and I. Sitting on the edge of the chair which scratches my bare legs where the starched white dress has ridden up, I stare at Mother but not directly, for even at this young age I have already learned her oblique sideways look by which to observe without being observed. I chart with every nerve each move she makes – adjusting the binoculars in her hand, recrossing her legs, flicking away a fly with her scarf. It is as if I live within her like the spirits old Gitende has described who inhabit trees, and yet she does not feel my presence though I gnaw at her relentlessly. I want far more than I can ever have; I am starving, hot-eyed, while she is cool, oblivious to need.

How can I be her child with such discrepancy? Yet I am, and incompatibility can only be my fault, my failing, but I cannot correct it; I am what I am, always hungry, always angry. Her bad child, the one she never wanted.

(I see that I have used the present tense automatically. Even now, sixty years later, even after all that has occurred, I can only think of Mother in the present tense. However, the present does not narrate and the past to tell its story must revert to the past.)

Mother was doing what she always did at breakfast – bird-watching; scanning the reed-fringed lake shore and floating islands of papyrus for water birds. Snowy-white egrets, herons, black ducks, crested grebes, cormorants, spoonbills. She never lost interest in their morning feeding activities, migrations, mating habits. While I watched her avid straight-backed position darkly, jealously, relentlessly, as if my intensity might turn her, draw away her alert absorption from those stupid, unworthy bundles of muscle and feather to me. There was genuine pain in all this, the sharp anguish of loneliness, for without Mother I had no one – and I was without Mother, all the time. Birdwatching was symbolic of the way her keen involvement with others, other people and animals, so rigidly excluded me. How I hated the dark tunnels of those binoculars which channelled her vision away from me and kept it there. At the age of three or four I tried to throw them into the lake, or so I was told; the ayah stopped me, all the servants laughed. I remember the incident differently: a huge bird, no doubt a vulture, came down from the sky and snatched the binoculars away. Profoundly grateful to it, nonetheless until recently I have loathed all birds automatically, a prejudice triggered solely by emotional memory.

On this particular morning the lake was lead grey and glassy, a mirror surface occasionally broken by the hump of a hippo. A few pale shades of pink and lemon yellow remained in the sky behind the hills, which were black silhouettes awaiting detail and wreathed in floating wisps of cloud. It was the rainy season – it would rain in the afternoon. The lawn stretching down to the lake shore was intensely green, iridescent and glistening with dew. A ring-tailed mongoose skittered across the edge of the garden where a line of jacarandas kept back the red-barked acacias; otherwise all was silence and still expectation: vegetation awaiting the day's downpour, the lake resting before the next storm.

I was still and expectant, hardly breathed in my chair. I detected something in the human atmosphere, I was tense with a sense of possibility, and felt, the way children can, omnipotent and directorial. Something was about to break the morning's immobility and I wanted it to happen, wanted it dreadfully, had to have it happen – though without any idea of what 'it' might be. So I know I connived at what happened next between my parents, not in any obvious way, but simply by being there and willing a climax; for there is a power in me of hidden manipulation which makes me responsible for every turn of events.

Mother put down her binoculars at last and wiped them

with a cobweb-thin silk scarf from round her neck. The delicacy of the scarf hurt me, as if Mother had used a piece of her own skin in such a careless way. I thought of her skin as silk; it looked so silky smooth and pale with luminosity, secretly flooded with life's activity well behind the visible exterior. Which was beautiful.

I have to say that I have never seen another woman as beautiful as Mother. Others did not exactly call her such: 'handsome' was the commonest description but never 'pretty' which would have been an insult – for she was unique, inimitable, one of a kind. And this I call beauty. This, and a sense of visual harmony, meaning that every part of the person in question enhances every other part. Most people appear to me quite disjointed, angular, asymmetrical, half-finished – which annoys and displeases my sense of aesthetics. Mother, on the other hand, was a finished work of art; perfection. The fact that I hated her never dulled my ardent appreciation, albeit reluctant and begrudged. Admiration, on the other hand, added fuel to my frustration – finding Mother beautiful in no way eased my resentment and anger; rather, it enhanced it.

She was tall for a woman and slim; rather feline and deliberate in her movements, every one of which was perfectly calculated, no waste, no mistakes, no inelegancies. She went about her life each day with armour-plated poise which was, for me, a wall of ice – and how I hammered at it, how I slipped and fell again and again as I tried to scale her heart. She gave me nothing to grip, gave nothing away, and though I burned against her year after year she was not to be melted: there was simply no way in.

Of course, she was aloof and cold-blooded with everyone. It was simply her way, her manner, and one which, I suppose, owed something to the fashions of the 'twenties and her youth. She would sit sideways in company, head thrown back in profile as she smoked deliberately and rather disdainfully, apparently totally remote, and yet always there, listening closely, watching others with slow sideways looks down her cheekbones. There may initially have been some degree of calculation in this mannerism because she appeared at her best in profile. It showed off her aquiline nose, regal forehead, the thickness of her dark hair which she never cut despite fashion and wore rolled up on the back of her neck. Full-face her eyes were a deep, Celtic blue, almost too intense a colour for comfort, and her eyebrows were arched in supercilious surprise, her lips painted red into a lovely, untouchable bow. She was highly conscious of appearances, never without the basic essentials of make-up, and superbly elegant in dress. The way she looked was as pristine as her self-control, as smooth and perfect and unassailable. Though I hated this as much as I admired it – I would search for a hair out of place or a ladder in her silk stockings – most people were impressed, indeed seduced, by such immaculate good taste.

Even at breakfast she dressed to be seen. On this particular morning she was wearing what she normally wore at that time of day: corduroy riding breeches (made for her by an Indian tailor in Nairobi) and a brightly coloured flannel shirt. Green it was, jade green, and I remember that because the silk scarf she wore was red, and red and green in juxtaposition have always disturbed me.

On this day, my birthday, I knew that Mother was disturbed. A rare, most unusual occurrence – it was this which had excited and alerted me. Though she would never let me into her thoughts, I saw in to a certain extent sometimes. I saw shadow patterns through ice, strange fluctuations of inner light. These were quite abnormal, a brief pathological flickering, for she was too strong, too indomitable to feel doubt. Yet doubt it was; doubt, fear and uncertainty. I knew that well before she started speaking, because she had eaten nothing, hardly even sipped her tea. She lit a cigarette, inhaled deeply and turned away into profile. Then she started.

'Tommy,' she said in her rainy day voice, which was chilly, translucent, deliberate. 'Tommy, what an odious tie you have on. Whatever for, my dear? I do so hope you'll think to change it before our guests come.'

'Guests?' Said as a half-question, half-statement. We so often had guests that it should hardly surprise him. I glanced towards the shadows where my father sat and found him more shadowy than ever, an indeterminate outline which was slightly ominous. I cannot remember him as anything more than a tall figure and a moustache, but then I have never been able to see men clearly as individuals, just as many people cannot see character in dogs. Men have always seemed to me a different species, and one not entirely to be trusted, unlike dogs. They do not endure; it is women who are history, the past and future of the species, race or family. Humans are naturally matriarchal and it has always seemed to me absurd that anyone should ever think otherwise.

'Is it possible, my dear, that our little party has slipped your mind? It seems odd that your memory can be quite so short when I reminded you only yesterday.' The words were light snowflakes, a feathery coating of frozen remarks.

But a storm was to follow. She was angry. Angry because she was disturbed. About something. Her anger was simmering; it had yet to burst the surface of her smooth, averted face.

Mother's anger was as rare as orchids in the forest, yet a constant possibility; the seeds were always there, lying dormant. Terrible to others, it was, I believe, also terrible to her as a temporary form of insanity, the ultimate loneliness. When it occurred it was so much at variance with her normal behaviour that I was led to believe everyone carries around in him his opposite characteristics – the gentle are cruel, the weak are strong. And the imperturbable can explode into uncontrollable fury.

These unusual rages both appalled and fascinated me. While I looked for small flaws, never found, here was destruction of her entire personality. And at my command – for it was usually me who made her angry; me, the bad child she consistently locked out of her mind – she would be suddenly enveloped by all the rage she never showed, never even knew she thought. I

22

were fixed on Mother. I was eating in every moment of dread, gorging myself on the rawness of it all, waiting for blood – my privilege and my punishment as the secret author of it all.

Mother exploded. Finally. In an act of silent dislocation and demise. She shot to her feet and swayed like a tall ebony tree about to crash down on us. Something happened to her beautiful face. It looked ripped apart from within, all the parts of it hanging useless, ugly without integrity. And I knew that her mind was the same, blown to pieces.

The time it took Mother to bring words to her lips was time enough for me to destroy one whole flower; the amputated petals I rubbed together in my damp palms.

'How dare you, Tom! How dare you! You have no right, none whatsoever to use Hermione in this way. I simply will not have it.'

'What won't you have, Matty?' Now he was drawling, deliberately.

I rubbed the petals, harder, harder, to make them bleed, to make my palms bleed. My parents were quarrelling about me though I could not quite tell why; the unknown reasons, unstated, were terrifying. Yet I wanted the outcome, I awaited a climax with hard, ardent elation.

'I won't have you claiming Hermione when she means nothing to you. Forgotten her birthday! Of course you have. A very appropriate slip of the memory, I dare say.' The way I had shredded the flower, she was shredding a piece of cake with rapid, desperate fingers; it had happened to be where her hands reached the table.

'Why, my darling?' He was slouching again, provocatively, one riding boot crossed negligently over the other; he felt himself to have the advantage now that she was mad. Her standing position was her isolation and her vulnerability.

I saw something like a wave move across her face. With hindsight I can only suppose it was the decision to say what she said next.

Which was: 'An appropriate slip because Hermione's birth-day is nothing to do with you. Because you had nothing to do with her birth. Her conception is what I am talking about.' A moment's pause. Then her voice became rapid and irritable, tired out, finished with the whole situation. 'Oh, for heaven's sake, must I spell it out. Hermione is not your child.'

My father reacted with uncharacteristic speed. He sprang forward, boots pounding the floor. He grabbed Mother's arm and began to bend her backwards as if he would snap her in two. I was not surprised by his violence; his voice, too cajoling, had always been that way. I watched and waited for Mother to win. She was after all defending me, and in this no one could defeat her – pretty or not, I was hers.

She reached behind her and grabbed at my father's hunting rifle which he had left propped up by the stairs, ready for his morning ride. She swung it round like a club and hit him a blow across the neck. He drew back, amazed, and in the space that opened up between them she raised it to her shoulder with the muzzle directed at his heart.

'Leave us,' she said.

And he did. As he slowly descended the stairs to the drive, and I could see him in profile behind Mother's profile, light glistened on his moustache as if it were wet with saliva or tears. He was very straight like a soldier as he walked away, but what I saw of him I saw through Mother because it was her I was watching, and she stood straighter than he did.

Then we were alone, Mother and I, as if for the very first time. Suddenly I was overwhelmed with a tremendous sense of triumph heightened by unfamiliar, unmanageable joy. She had done it all for me: shown feeling, proven care. She had fought my father on my behalf, sent him away for my sake; for our sake so that it might be just the two of us as it was always meant to be. The distance between us, her chilly remoteness, for this brief space of time seemed an illusion, and I knew instead that she loved me and had always loved me. The thought was narcotic. I soared on the upcurrent of illusory hope, I floated above us like a drunken angel.

But I needed reassurance. Only a child, I required support to keep flying.

I awaited a move from her. Some sign. The world outside was full of signs: the sun appeared over the edge of the hills as a huge, brilliant star of pure yellow. It was warm, Mother need never grow cold again; our day was beginning in tropical bliss. But Mother did not see the sun, she looked into the shadows where my father had been sitting. Her hair had come loose and hung in ropes like dying snakes draped down her back.

When she finally spoke it was into empty space. 'The ducklings have hatched.'

A dreadful, mad remark meaning nothing; there was nothing between us after all. I had waited in vain. I was wrong. On the verge of achieving that thing, her love, which I most wanted, which was mine by rights, I was left with nothing, again left with nothing. Again abandoned and alone.

I fell badly. I leapt off my chair, wiped my hands on my pinafore and screamed at Mother. My face was contorted, the skin stretched to breaking point; my features were coming apart, all those bits of me which looked like her, and they would never reassemble into anything whole and harmonious, worth looking at. I was ugly. I screamed, first a terrible bellow then specific words.

'I hate you and I'll never forgive you.'

This was the first time I had said 'hate' to her. Having said it, it was true for ever whereas hate unspoken had been a form of hope, a plea. Twisting my head away from what I had done, I glanced down at my pinafore and noticed a purple stain from the mangled petals smeared across my heart.

As for my father, he never came back.

THREE

❧❧❧❧❧❧❧❧❧❧❧❧❧❧❧❧❧

Mother had said that I was not my father's child. At the time
I did not understand what she meant – I presumed it a way of
undermining his authority by reminding him that she shared
in possession of me – and it was only much later that I realised
the issue was one of paternity, physical origins, co-authorship
of my genetic make-up. Had she meant what she said or was
it simply a desperate ploy, the last and cruellest weapon she
could find to use against him?

I decided that it must be the latter. In the height of anger
Mother often said strange things which seemed to have little
bearing on reality, yet expressed her intentions most forcibly.
Anyway, I must be Tom Goodenough's child by reason of a
simple logic: she did not love me, so I must derive from a man
she did not love. In rejecting him, she rejected me, and when
he walked away for ever she denied my desperate requirements
because I was part of him. Though there was more to it than
that; my sins ran deeper. There was something else in me that
only she could see, a crime I was born with which kept her
away. When she was angry she saw it, her gaze showed dreadful
insight. But I never knew, could only guess at ugliness; and
guessing made it worse, both the crime and my fear of it, and
my anger and resentment at all I could not control. I had never
asked for this – never wished to be born in the first place,
regardless of who my natural parents might be.

Strange as it may seem, I hardly cared about paternity. When
my father left I did not mourn him, I was mildly relieved to
be able to forget him. Irrelevant was what he was: I felt it

unlikely that a man had had as much to do with my conception as they are meant to, so strong was my sense of issuing from Mother and from her alone. In my mind there were only two people, her and me; no room then for a shadowy third to complicate the straightforward way I hated her.

I never told my sister Angela about the 'not your child' thing. Not even when I left home and was living with her and her husband in London. I always felt that it was none of her business, and it wasn't. She, for her part, had missed our father greatly when he so suddenly vanished from our lives, and managed, after her marriage, to track him down in South America. Though they never met again they corresponded until he died. She wanted me to write too – I refused outright: 'Don't be so bloody absurd. You are a fool, Angela. What has he ever done for us, buggering off the way he did, leaving Mother in the lurch with two small children? Can't think that we owe him a thing, not even the odd obscene postcard.' But still she wrote, religiously.

She was rather obsessed with fathers, was poor old Angela. When I became engaged to Olaf, her first comment was: 'But H-H-Hermione' (she always tripped up badly on my name), 'he is old enough to be your f-father.'

Technically she was quite right, of course; I was only eighteen and he was thirty-five. But I felt much older than my years – had I not after all proved old and cold enough to engineer my escape from Mother two years earlier? And I was working, on and off, earning pin money by typing and modelling hats. I was a viable adult, which Olaf's affection only confirmed. I accused Angela of objecting to my marriage for other reasons.

'For heaven's sake, you might at least be honest. It's class that's bothering you. You think he's not good enough for me, not a gentleman such as Mother would approve of.' (The idea that Mother might be shocked by Olaf excited me, spurred me on.) 'I shall feel sorry to think that you lack the intelligence to see deeper than appearances. Typical, isn't it? The English are such snobs.'

'But you are English too, H-H-Hermione. That's just the point. W-will you be happy with an American? Or Norwegian, or whatever he is. And can he take care of you? What if s-something goes wrong?'

'If something goes wrong, I shall do what I always do: get out a crossword puzzle, it soothes the mind.'

I seem to hear Angela sobbing at this point; she was pregnant and particularly emotional – which was hardly surprising considering the state of her marriage. A few months later the child was born dead, but by that time I was already in America with Olaf. It was another seven years before Angela became pregnant again, this time with Nicola.

I can find no pity in my voice for Angela; it would seem that even now I cannot feel it. Rivals into the grave. I can only suppose that I've never forgiven her for issuing from Mother, and three years before me. I always felt like an only child; Angela proved otherwise, and contradicted other basic beliefs about Mother and myself, and the state of the world in general. Put simply, we did not get along.

Angela was both right and wrong about Olaf. He was an odd choice of mate – a huge, ungainly, bald individual, under-educated and uncultured; the son of Norwegian immigrant farmers. When we met he was attached to the RAF, but after war broke out that autumn he was recalled to the United States, taking me with him as his wife. There he was given administrative duties throughout the war, and afterwards left the Air Force to set up his own air freight company in Montana. Angela needn't have worried about me becoming a financial burden on her household again – Olaf took good care of me. His business prospered and he treated me well in every respect.

I think it safe to say that Olaf loved me. At least, he said he did, though I could never imagine what it was he saw in me exactly. After all, he had no idea what went on in my mind – and that was the beauty of it from my point of view: the privacy, the freedom, of living with someone who could not possibly understand me, while at the same time providing calm and secure protection. Which I badly needed in those newly independent years, strange though it may seem and seemed to others – Angela considered me a tower of bullying strength. But I realized I was still vulnerable and that whatever my true strength might be, I had not yet matured to it.

In a manner of speaking, marriage was a means of convalescence from my childhood. But this approach to matrimony is not so very unusual; I remember that someone once told me about a Cambridge maths graduate, a woman, married most contentedly to a bargeman on the Thames who treated her with great kindness and respect. So, too, my Olaf. Like the bargeman he took me far away from my past until there was half a world between Mother and me. Geographical distance was essential to recovery. As well as the language barrier between Olaf and myself; we spoke different languages and I wanted it that way because communication would have torn me, shredded my nerves. The last thing I needed was intelligent sympathy.

Poor Olaf realized none of this. He thought me a good wife, thought I did the job well. He was proud of my looks, so perhaps it was some idea of beauty which he loved. He admired my way of walking in high heels, my long dark hair (which I refused to cut or curl) and my autocratic profile. 'Just like a queen or a duchess,' he would say. 'Hermie, you sure are swell.' After the war, he brought me home to his parents in Montana like a wonderful prize, a gift from the gods so special that he knew he hardly deserved it. (His parents also knew that he hardly deserved me – deserved much better, in fact.)

He built our house outside of Billings himself, added to it as money started coming in, took great pride in its facilities and crafted surfaces. A castle, he called it, fit for a queen. I ruled there easily, recreating some of the rituals from Kenyan life though without such accessories as servants, Limoges china, good crystal, crested silverwear. Not that Olaf didn't try to buy me such things. He did his best to surround me with objects which might remind me of home, though his natural taste in such things was laughable: dime-store plastics were his passion – he could see no point in having things which break or tarnish. He was better on more intimate items; bought me silk stockings and good scent when he flew to New York on business, or sent me to Denver on shopping trips for decent clothes. Whatever I wanted he wanted for me.

I was his child and he wished to display me to advantage. Proud of my skills at entertaining, he liked to bring colleagues home, or take me into town for social events organized by the Rotary Club. Ridiculous, really, but I was capable of patience. A foreigner in self-chosen exile I did enough to win respect and tolerance without fitting, for if I fitted I would no longer be foreign. I had no women friends in all those years and never missed them. There were a few men. There was Rick who let me ride his horses; he called me 'the Duchess' and chuckled at my straight-backed English way of riding. But his humour hid awe which kept in check the way his eyes slid around my thighs and his hands quivered slightly as he helped me up into the saddle. When Olaf suggested we move into town and I refused – I needed isolation – he thought, and I could see it in his eyes, that Rick might be the reason. Nothing of the kind. No attraction there, not on my part.

I have never felt what other women indicate they feel when they talk about men. I do not say this as confession; it is quite immaterial to me one way or the other that I've never felt erotic passion. So what? Do monks miss sex? Does anyone miss what he's never had? There are so many ways in which one might be lacking that the absence of eager sexuality seems to me still a very small deficit and not much to be regretted. Yes, it is the other things I regret; the larger deficiencies, the ones which can never be entirely self-forgiven.

A selfless, helpless husband, there was nonetheless one thing which Olaf wanted for himself, though he said that he wanted it for me. A baby. And on this one enormous issue my confidence in him foundered, and all the distance I had carefully sustained between us proved justified. He was devious with peasant cunning in his efforts to achieve his heart's desire, and by betraying me to get it he undid all the good he had done.

Olaf knew how much I was against having children. I had the dogs, they were my children, and I was Olaf's child – no room here for natural progeny. But the issue was more serious, ran deeper: I had never asked to be born, still less had I asked to perpetuate myself beyond one life. I knew it was wrong that I should ever have children, that I was a carrier of something, some psychogenic virus or inherited defect of the emotions. I also knew that because I hated Mother I would hate anything that made me a mother; and this proved true, very much so. Poor Susan. She never asked for life either.

She was Olaf's fault completely. He had taken responsibility for avoiding such 'accidents'; which made me know that she was no accident. He made her happen despite my resolute rejection of motherhood. Olaf guessed that I was pregnant even before I told him – further proof that she was there by his design.

From then until Susan's birth he treated me as if I were an invalid or a precious piece of china about to break; such care and solicitousness, and how it infuriated me. 'For God's sake, Olaf,' I would say, 'must you pussyfoot about the place? And don't make me tea. The last pot you brewed was perfectly frightful.'

He would reply to such comments with honest, inappropriate looks of deep appreciation; he always liked the sound of my voice, called it 'growling', meaning deep and gravelly. Nearly a man's voice, he said, and this seemed to attract him like a siren's song. He never listened to what I said, just to my voice.

'Oh, for heaven's sake, can't you just toddle off somewhere? If you leave me alone I shall take up the prone position like a good girl. If you don't, I'm off riding.'

That threat always upset him. He would come over and smother me in his kind bear's embrace, trying to explain. 'It's just that I'm kinda worried 'bout you, Hermie. You and the kid. I'm real happy, and real scared too that something might go wrong.'

'Like what? Which one of us are you most afraid of losing?'

I was so very angry. Rage and loneliness clouded my vision to everything but the absolute unfairness of his bald head beaming its good intentions, while the child inside me lay absolutely still as if she heard me willing her to die. Olaf abandoned me, my old self, when he made me pregnant and kept me a prisoner of my body. To be more exact, I felt a prisoner of his, as if I were the one entombed in a womb, his, and I kicked and scratched and fought to be free. It hurt him. He aged considerably during those miserable nine months.

He aged even more afterwards under the burden of motherhood. I say 'motherhood' because he took over from me with Susan very early on. Breastfeeding was not for me (nor did anyone promote it much in those days) and I needed my sleep. Olaf took over the four-hourly feeds, and the nappies, and did it gladly, joyfully. He would show the baby off to me a way I suppose some women do who have had babies to keep the marriage together; there was something pleading and intransigent, desperate and blind to the uselessness of it all when he showed me new teeth, how she looked in pretty dresses, or exclaimed at how cleverly she crawled. Not that I didn't know any of this – after all, I had to take care of Susan when he went to work – but he told me such things the way neglected wives will, to win attention and elicit guilt, pretending I might not notice as protest against my not caring.

He once tried to explain to me what he thought he was

doing. 'There'll be someone here to love you, Hermie, when I'm long gone. This little girl's gonna love you a lot, I know it, and that's what I want. You need it, Hermie. You need more love than most folks do, just like pups weaned too early.'

'Never cared much for mother's milk myself, but still.' Cool and haughty, I pivoted on my heels, balancing myself with one hand behind me on the piano. Then I exploded. 'How dare you talk to me that way! Such stupid, sentimental slush. You have no right, none whatsoever to play saint with me. I simply won't have it!'

I was always too strong for him: his big shoulders collapsed and his head fell forward like a boulder crashing down a cliff edge. His bald pate was as dull as old pewter but I felt no pity. He had deserted me. Everything he did now was for Susan.

Olaf died when Susan was eight. A heart attack whilst out duck shooting. He needn't have gone, I blamed Susan – she was so eager to be out at the beginning of the season, she begged him to take her. And as he never refused her slightest wish, and never went anywhere without her, off they went at five in the morning to be in position by dawn. Perhaps it was the cold – huge columns of snow swept towards them across the lake – or perhaps it was simply the excitement as they lay in their boat near the shore, eyes fixed on the decoys and scanning the sky. Suddenly Olaf slumped down and Susan knew at once that something was wrong. When he would not move or talk she set off to find help and came upon another group of hunters returning to their cars. By the time they got him home he was dead.

I looked down at his grey face and red eyelids locked tight against ever seeing me again. There was a moment when something twisted in me, an unbearable emotion which I hardly knew but which knew me.

I went over to pick up a brace of bleeding mallards which the hunters had left behind – a gift or forgetfulness? I put them in the sink, vaguely aware that Susan was behind me, clinging to my skirt and sobbing. I glanced at her face which was beseeching and expectant, a watery moon turned upwards to latch onto my gaze. She pulled at me, trying to draw us together. 'What beautiful ducks,' I commented, and stroked their green necks. Iridescent green, the colour of the lawn at Naivasha during the rains. Though I said this to Susan, and meant it truthfully as clear communication and the most I could say to her, a direct speech from my heart to hers – the most I had ever given her and close to what I ought to feel and maybe did – yet she must have thought my words an evasion because the drag of her weight on my skirt immediately subsided. And I felt far too light, I felt abandoned.

With the ducks' wings stiff under my hands, stretched out, flying from death, I called out to Mother across half the world and two decades of separation. I called out, I hate you and I'll never forgive you. I blamed her, blamed her bitterly for the fact that I was once again alone.

I had never realized that Olaf was close company until I lost him. So is that love? A question of definition I suppose. My need for him ran deep, and need is attachment, and attachment is . . . a kind of love. For most of my life I have thought of myself as unloving, and blamed Mother. But now I am kinder to myself, and a little indifferent, at least from time to time; such as today, with the long rains just started and a keen sense of release from the oppressive heat, and so I can release myself from that one particular remorse and say, yes, in your own way you loved Olaf. Darling, you did the best you could.

I had Olaf buried beneath a large maple tree at the end of our property where I buried the dogs. Later when I sold off land he had to be relocated in a public cemetery.

Susan was less easily solved. Nothing went well with her after her father died. It seemed to me that, quite literally, she could not live without him. Not properly, at any rate. She ran wild without being wild, like a feral dog which still comes back for feeding and for patting, begging to be given whatever it was the lack of which first sent it away. This frustrated and infuriated me: the child had no backbone, no integrity, little intelligence; I had never begged and when I left I left for good – not so with Susan.

I found it hard to believe that Susan was my child. There was nothing in her that I recognized, no messages from the past, no solutions in her glance; I looked like Mother but Susan did not look like me or her grandmother – there was nothing there for me to love or hate. Had the hospital made a mistake? Not likely, because she closely resembled the female line in Olaf's family: squat, thick-set, gingery women bred for hard labour and childbearing. It sometimes seemed to me as if Olaf had had Susan all by himself, some masculine form of immaculate conception, and I had been nothing but a carrier, a temporary nest for this cuckoo's egg and its unappealing issue. The snag in the system was that I was left with her, the one who loved her gone, and she, for her part, was incapable of taking to wing and leaving her false mother, which was surely the decent and self-respecting thing to do. After all, I did it.

Susan did poorly at school, began to spend all her time with youths with slicked-back greasy hair and noisy cars as soon as her breasts were obvious enough to attract them. And attract them she did. There was an abortion at fifteen – the first of many expensive efforts on my part to get her out of trouble. Her friends were petty criminals; nothing strenuous or imaginative, just purse snatching, joy-riding in stolen cars, the occasional easy break-in. And Susan went along with these activities in a mindless, passive fashion; she was less of a delinquent than an empty vessel for the use of other delinquents.

Which enraged me more than her actual activities, for if she was to be so readily moulded by other wills, then why not by mine? Why not let me fill her with strength, stubbornness, determination; admirable qualities and the essence of survival. Weak people can learn to appear strong, but she refused my lessons, the only kind I was able to give, and consequently every failure in her life was yet another monotonous demonstration of her rejection of me. I blamed her for the ruin that her life became – waitressing jobs, quickly lost or left, the same of men. Even her marriage lasted barely two years, just time enough to conceive two children she could not support – more responsibility for me. And I would look at this child-woman who was supposed to be mine, yet who was nothing like me and so alien in appearance, and I would think: you are doing this on purpose, you are punishing me. I blamed her for being a permanent fixture in my life, yet not part of it, not part of me. I felt lonelier when she was there than when she was not, and blamed her.

Susan half left home gradually from the age of sixteen, first spending nights away with boyfriends, then sharing shacks or caravans and only coming back to live with me whenever her domestic arrangements broke down, or the plumbing, or it got too cold in winter. Regardless of where she happened to be staying she always came to visit at least once a week. Sometimes it seemed to me that the lack of common bonding between us held her tighter to me than genuine maternal affection ever would have done.

She would turn up at my side and wait there silently, some gift in her hands: poached fish, stolen fruit, flowers from someone else's garden. I avoided her eyes; the beseeching look there, too raw to be dog-like yet just as devoted, and totally vulnerable – one glance and the guilt and the anger it caused me would use up my courage for the day. She would never speak until I gave some indication that I noticed her.

'I didn't want to disturb you, Mom,' she would say, which irritated me by its lack of self-assertion, and, I thought, hidden reproach. Unfair. Was I really so formidable, so aloof, so indifferent to her presence that she dared not speak without permission?

'Oh, for heaven's sake, honey, must you pussyfoot about the place? Announce yourself properly when you arrive, it's just the thing one does. God knows my hearing is not what it used to be – just give me a clue to your presence so I don't die of fright.'

To which she would reply, quite predictably, 'Ah, Mom, you shouldn't say such things.' No sense of humour had Susan then, no wit or irony in her speech and understanding; like a marshmallow – sticky and nothing bites back.

At the time of Christmas in London with Nicola, just after Mother's death, Susan was about to turn thirty. I felt that her lifestyle was becoming terminal; she could not go on as she was for much longer. I hoped, almost superstitiously, that Nicola or her husband might in some way provide a solution. The time would come when I was not around, having chosen freedom in one form or another: death or moving house. I never meant to be a mother yet stayed one longer than most, but there were limits and natural conclusions to the stages of life, or unnatural ones. Whatever, something had to be done about Susan.

Yet she was no more than a speck on the periphery, a very minor character in my thoughts during the long flight across the Atlantic. It was family I was thinking of, my real family. And those many years between leaving home and the present intractable fact of Mother's death – the years of my marriage and of motherhood – seemed inconsequential and not quite real. Rather like a working holiday prior to returning home. Indeed, it is significant that even today those forty years give back so little detail, while the times before and after map out the substance of my life.

Flying to Nicola felt like flying home. She was all that was left of it now, and I realized, on that plane ride, that I had always meant to do just this, return home, yet left it too late.

FOUR

❧❧❧❧❧❧❧❧❧❧❧❧❧❧❧❧❧❧❧

When I first caught sight of Nicola by the arrivals' barrier at Heathrow, I hardly recognized her. She looked like a ghost, by which I mean that she seemed not entirely alive; not as much as she ought to be, or used to be. And she was pale, rather drawn, appearing older than her thirty-five years – but that I put down to neon lighting (wretched stuff, installed indiscriminately in public places to make women look like hags). The other thing I noticed at once about Nicola, in those first few seconds of recognition, was an air of isolation, despite the crowds around, and I was reminded of the faces of refugees caught between countries, with no home and little hope. She looked desolate, as if her eyes, fixed beyond the stream of travellers pushing trolleys, were watching in the distance her own demise. Certainly she seemed aware of nothing going on around her, she was locked into herself; she would never see me – I waved.

I have always believed in first impressions. Mine are normally acute and accurate. Yet, as I gesticulated to gain Nicola's attention, and her face instantly changed, coloured, livened, I decided I was wrong, deluded; too tired by travel to see things properly. Or maybe only seeing a version of myself.

She pushed forward in the awkward, erratic way people who always move slowly are forced into when they rush. I thought, she's glad to see me; though her first words were rambling fragments of politeness which might have been sprinkled on anyone. 'Oh, I am so pleased and . . . super . . . so dreadfully tiring, I do hope that . . .'

Nicola dropped bits of sentences the way some people drop

Kleenex. She never noticed the loss of them, nor looks of perplexity from uninitiated listeners. Once one got to know her well her incomplete comments were as full and meaningful as anyone else's, if not more so, and the parts left out seemed a tender show of trust – that one understood her well enough to read between the spasmodic words her deepest thoughts; in consequence of which her utterances were wreathed in hidden significance interpreted according to what the listener wished to hear. It sometimes seemed as if she were more foreign to her own tongue than any foreigner could be, and yet so mightily familiar with it that, like a poet, abbreviations and odd liaisons were her prerogative; her right, indeed, to unique delivery.

I found her speech charming, quite delightful to the ear. Her voice itself was a little bit breathy as if not quite under control, and would indeed reach unduly high or low notes in wrong places – another source of mystification. This made one listen to her more closely than to other people; she commanded attention the way whisperers do.

I kissed the first cheek I reached. 'Nicola, darling, you look wonderful. Very well indeed.'

'Really? I . . . but you look so elegant, Hermione, quite like . . . and Mummy always used to tell me how wonderfully you dress, just like Matty, so perfect . . . of course, I do love your jewellery, pearls are very fashionable not that I . . .'

Not that she followed fashion. Nicola cultivated an air of frugality which, I'm afraid, was more natural than contrived. She looked like a bag lady run rampant at the end of a charity sale, adorned with all the curious bits and pieces no one would buy at any low price. I am sure she dressed only in handouts though her husband could well afford designer labels.

'What's this you're wearing, darling? You haven't been debagging monks, have you?' I fingered her over-garment which resembled a priest's hooded robe, and reminded me of the capuchins lepers wore to hide their disfigurements.

'Super, isn't it . . . yes, Morocco, I should think, though . . .'

And, leading the way, she glided off in front of me like a drifting cloud, unhurried, direction not obvious, her long black cloak catching at her heels where bits of something mauve and wispy showed beneath its tattered hem.

I was amused. I like individuality (it used to exasperate me mightily the way Susan copied the fashions of her peers with no mind of her own) and I believe it fair to say that I have always accepted anyone who can interest me. Had Nicola not been my closest relative she would nonetheless have intrigued me pleasantly, alerted my curiosity. I would always have wanted to know her.

There was something just slightly theatrical about Nicola, as if calculated to provide gentle entertainment. She was so vague and ethereal, so wafting, to the point of becoming a caricature of herself; just as her speech was very nearly disastrous. There were moments when I wondered: did she do this on purpose, was it all just a game, an act, a cover-up for something else? And of course it was the 'something else' which I was after and which I knew to be family: inherited characteristics, the basic things she shared with me and no one else. Anger, isolation, inspiration: I knew it must all be there though her behaviour revealed nothing of the kind.

She was extremely mild-mannered in an absent-minded sort of way, always pleasant and half-smiling as though she had forgotten exactly what amused her but knew that presently she would be amused again, so kept the smile in readiness. She tended to look off into the distance, dreamily, with her head back and her long, delicate nose in the air; and glide from the room in this abstracted fashion with her eyes apparently lost in details on the ceiling. Blue eyes, a little darker than Mother's, less disturbing, and softly shuttered by sleepy, fragile eyelids shadowed violet which were never wide open or quite closed. She had long dark hair which she wore in a single braid down her back where it swayed or reposed like a creature with a life of its own. Where her hair was pulled back long earrings tended to dangle down and catch at her shoulders; sometimes she only wore one, or two which did not match, though whether these irregularities were deliberate I could never tell.

However one looked at her, Nicola was eccentric. Different, not one of the crowd. She reminded me somewhat of Virginia Woolf without the madness and the genius. It was, I suppose, Nicola's tragedy that she was unusual but not exceptional. A flaw which runs in the family: we have none of us proved able to achieve our heart's desire.

This encounter was my second meeting with Nicola. I never knew her as a child, what with Angela and me continents apart and unwilling to risk money and emotional stability on long journeys to meet.

Nicola did not have what might be termed a stable upbringing. Her father – hand-picked by Mother as an excellent 'catch' – was an alcoholic, a womanizer and a dishonest businessman who was always in debt and only by good fortune not in jail. What security there was in the household was provided by Angela who was hardly a pillar of strength, always ill and anxious, and too indecisive to provide solutions of her own. For several years running, when times were particularly hard, she sent Nicola home to Mother during the English summer; 'home' by then being a bungalow on the beach just outside of Dar es Salaam.

Those were the good times, as Nicola saw it; the bad times were her adolescent years when Angela turned from malingering to bed-ridden invalidism. She wrote to me about her ailments, at length and too frequently, and when one of them turned into cancer her tone was triumphant and relieved: at last, she wrote, I can rest. What else had she been doing for most of her life? Nicola took on the responsibility of running the house and tending to the needs of her mother in decline. The father had vanished, I can't remember when, nor probably did Nicola and Angela place his departure very exactly, considering that he was never around.

Nicola took up nursing when she left school. This seemed a most appropriate profession – after all, she had done nothing else for so many years. Yet when Angela finally died Nicola dropped her training. It was useless, she told me, all that medical know-how, and none of it relevant because medicine means healing, it caters to the curable not the terminally ill. Nothing helped Angela in the ways she most needed help: 'Mummy died badly' was how Nicola put it, and that simple description stuck in my mind.

Soon afterwards Nicola became very ill herself with some stomach ailment. (I think she might have said it was colitis – never ill myself until recently, I have had no patience with pathology; just as some cannot recall other people's names I have no memory for their diseases.) In hospital she met her husband, Augustus, who was the specialist assigned to her case. Had she remained his patient happily ever after? Nicola laughed when I said this to her on my last visit.

Which was the first time we met, two years before our Christmas reunion. I was coming through London on a tour of Europe forced upon me by Olaf's old colleagues in the Rotary Club. I had one night in London. I wrote to Nicola and she wrote back to insist that I spend it with them.

When we met I knew at once that I had been right to establish contact.

Blood is thicker than water: this woman carried aspects of me in her veins, I could feel it, I could see it, despite our obvious differences. I knew that we would have to meet again, and properly. We exchanged letters – so convenient, letters, more selective than conversation and less ambiguous; to be read at one's leisure and in one's own way – and from these I built up an accurate, detailed picture of Nicola which excitement had prevented at the time; so that, when Christmas was planned, I knew exactly to whom I was speaking. Knew her as well as I knew myself. I felt, although we had spent so little time together, that she was a life-long intimate and the only person in the world to whom I might turn, not exactly in need but to talk. I very nearly trusted her, when I had never trusted anything but dogs.

We stood in the taxi queue for rather a long time. Nicola wrapped the inadequate cloak tightly around her angular shoulders, and stood, sway-backed, like a misplaced comma, with one arm braced on the railing for support. From time to time she shivered, not a quiet trembling but a sudden juddering motion the way a car jerks when it stalls. Alarming, but quickly over. I buttoned up my mink coat; indeed, it was chilly.

Nicola fumbled in a secret pocket in her cloak and drew out a packet of cigarettes, lit one with a small, bright sheet of flame from a lighter. Momentarily her cheeks were red like raw wounds, then the light was gone, smoke drifted lovingly towards her hair, and her skin turned grey, pallid, as if the way she tilted back her head to inhale drained all the blood out of it.

'Darling, I didn't think you smoked, don't ask me why. I thought your husband was against all such unhealthy practices.'

She glanced at me obliquely in a way which was mildly conspiratorial. 'Yes, he . . . but you won't tell him, will you?'

Then she puffed away with odd, greedy vigour until her face was half shrouded in pearly smoke clouds, and her head seemed to float on them, and I was reminded uneasily of angels who are after all dead people. Perhaps I showed some anxiety, for she added, 'Not that I smoke very often, only when . . . and it is relaxing, you see, which outweighs . . . anyway, no point now in thinking about health, really.'

She gave a little painter-like flourish with her cigarette as if it were a brush, which reminded me that that was what she did: painting – she painted illustrations for books. In consequence of this unconscious gesture, ash fell inside her sleeve, and when she let her hand drop, it snowed out again as though the arm inside had been burnt away. Then, our thoughts being somehow conjoined, she gave reason to my morbid imagery by stating what was on her mind.

45

'You know, don't you, Hermione, how Matty . . . the exact manner, I mean, it was not what one would have wished for her as a means of departure, but then we rarely can choose, can we? I mean, can we choose? I would like to think, and I feel that I . . . but with her it was all purely accidental and . . .'

'An accident?'

'Well, you know how Matty smoked, one cigarette after the other when her hands were not occupied in any other . . . so she must have been just sitting up in bed and thinking, not reading, I mean, and it was . . . the mosquito net, they catch fire so easily, and then the flames spread.' Her purple eyelids had nearly closed to shut out, or shut in, what she told me.

I was cold with horror. 'Are you telling me that Mother was burnt to death?'

'Not exactly, at least . . . and I only know what Kumar . . . but the doctor did think she had a heart attack first, or during, so that pain is not so very likely and that is, of course, what one dreads, you know, the idea of dying in pain, because . . . I have always thought that ghosts could be explained that way, dying badly, you know, without peace to free the spirit. I believe very strongly in peace at the end, in things done properly, but . . . poor Matty.' Her long braid twitched on the funereal material of her cloak though I could see no explanation for its slight movement.

She looked at me insistently. Face on, her hooded eyes were paler, stronger. Keenly penetrating. Suddenly she was intense, not mild.

'I'm sure it must have been the heart attack that finished her. Anyone who smokes that much is automatically at risk.' I did not know what she wanted; I wished to draw her off.

She sighed; dropped the stub of her cigarette without seeming to notice its loss. Still alight it caught briefly on her cloak, then rolled off into the gutter. She folded her arms and arched her back again, eyes off somewhere in the sky, the clouds, catching after birds or departing aircraft. I realised, however, that she was concentrating on certain thoughts.

'It does run in the family, you know, fire, death by fire . . . fire at the time of death. There was her father as well . . . so I have wondered . . .'

'My grandfather?'

'Did Matty never tell . . . ?'

But this time there was reason for an incomplete sentence. It was our turn, finally, for a taxi.

We did not say much during the ride into London. Yawning, shivering, Nicola seemed more tired than I was, and she frequently looked away out of the window; then, as if afraid of seeming inattentive, she would flick her head around and make some brief, disjointed comment. I nodded, said nothing.

When the motorway came to an end at a large roundabout we were close to our destination. Perhaps the fact that the journey had few minutes left made her rush to express herself before entering the house, which was Augustus's and not neutral territory. At any rate, Nicola suddenly reached across and embraced me. Tightly. Like a child.

'I am so glad,' she said, 'and so grateful, so relieved, I feel that now I can begin to let go a little, and it will all . . . when you rang last month it was like fate, as if Matty . . . you do sound like her, you know, and how my heart leapt, I could hardly think let alone find words to say, I was so glad.'

'Me too, darling.'

Though I wondered about the rather desperate way she put things. Why should she be desperate? – she wasn't me. As for the comparison with Mother, this mystified me, for surely we sounded totally different, my voice was never so cold and heartless – peremptory perhaps but not frigid.

Nicola seemed to wish to deny her impromptu demonstration of affection. Her next comment was about the weather. 'It really might snow, the weatherman said so last night, and tomorrow too, if . . . but of course one never knows.'

'Don't ask me why. After all, birds do, and most animals.'

'Do you like . . . ?'

'Animals? Dogs, yes, and horses. Most animals for that matter – I had so many pets when I was young. But I loathe birds.'

'Strange, really, considering that Matty . . . and her binoculars.'

'Exactly.'

'Ah, yes, you and Matty weren't exactly . . .' And she looked as if this were something she had forgotten because she doubted its validity.

'We weren't exactly friends. Quite right. I hated her.'

I had realized the last time we met that Nicola would never believe me on this; could not, because she loved Mother devotedly. And to evade the issue she did what Mother used to do: turned away into profile, her long nose rather sharp, less delicate in that position and rather autocratic. From there she swept me a quick, supercilious sideways look totally at odds with her habitually soft attitudes.

And all at once, for the very first time, she reminded me so strongly of Mother that I gasped, I went cold, I believe that the hair on the back of my neck stood on end. She was Mother exactly, was Nicola. Why had I not seen this before?

But I had, of course, without realizing it, and that was why I was here. Mother was dead but she had left behind an unlikely replica with whom I might construct a dialogue. So much unresolved between us, and the hatred which ought never to be kept beyond death – I had missed my chance, I had not gone home to be with Mother when she died. But fate, or God, or Mother herself was merciful; for here was Nicola, and she, somehow, must be my second chance.

I was halfway home.

FIVE

❧❧❧❧❧❧❧❧❧❧❧❧❧❧❧❧❧❧

That Nicola reminded me so closely of Mother ought not to have come as a surprise: there was no one else she could bring to mind because most people I simply do not remember; I carry away no image of them when they are not there. Olaf's face evaporated when he died, and even Susan I cannot see – and she was with me only recently. But Mother's face has always been clearer to me than memory, and more immediate, like a symbol – a star or a cross – the exact meaning of which nonetheless remains obscure.

My first glimpse of Nicola at the airport brought back to me, when I wrote about it later in my diary, my last glimpse of Mother as I left home, never to return. Mother taking her final sideways glance at me with a face so empty and desolate that she also looked like a refugee without hope, and I knew I was mistaken to see so much just as I knew I was wrong about Nicola. After all, Mother was indomitable, insane with confidence. She had never wanted me while I was her prisoner so why should she mourn my freedom?

Nonetheless she did. As I rode my pony away through the chill morning mist and the red oat grass, a flight of green parrots shot out of the cedar forest and anvil birds called and replied from a bamboo thicket – but I knew that her binoculars, as she sat on the verandah over breakfast, were trained on me. My departing back. Finally I had her intense, undivided attention, now that it was too late.

Tears spotted my cheeks like early warning of a downpour and soon I could see nothing ahead of me but a grey empty blur. I had done the cruellest thing I could possibly do, I had worse than killed her, and life ahead in consequence held little joy or horror. I could have reined in the pony and returned, and yet I could not. I was leaving for ever, a finite period of time the conclusion of which, like the expiry of some sentence of exile, would be revealed to me when I least expected it. But not now; there was no turning back, just as there had never been any undoing of my definitive statement: I hate you and I'll never forgive you. When tears strayed into my mouth it was her blood I tasted.

My last years with Mother, when we lived at Njoro, were a history of escalating conflict. Not that it would have appeared as such to an outside observer, for Mother with her impenetrable self-control was ostensibly above conflict. She never twitched an eyelid at my sullen, difficult behaviour – at its worst in front of guests, a calculated effort on my part to embarrass her. But when we were alone, completely private, with not even Angela present, then very occasionally her rage would erupt with emotion which reached out to tear me apart. Unable to elicit response when I wanted it, frantic for the most part to feel feeling, to know that her heart also beat, suddenly I was bombarded with more than I could manage, a deluge of wishes and meanings I could not understand, except as one conclusion: that she hated me.

It is the children who are not loved who become obsessed with their parents; or rather, the children who know they might have been loved, the potential was there yet never realized; because, while indifference breeds indifference, emotional incommunication breeds yearning which often looks back with the hard face of hatred. Had Mother not been angry I would never have hated her. I would have been careless, oblivious. And yet, it does seem to me to be every child's right to attach – animal young die if they cannot cling to their mothers – whereas Mother never allowed me the slightest handhold; so, I suppose, there was never any way out of obsession except love, that least likely possibility.

The strangest thing is that, despite the hiatus between us, in a dark and cloudy way I understood Mother; that is, I would comprehend and then instantly smash my comprehension. It was as if I possessed two layers of knowledge about her: loud and clear knowledge, my thoughts and my words, and then their shadows which took a different form, full of sorrow. For example, I could never say 'Mother cried when I left' even though my every description of our parting runs with tears.

Each day at Njoro commenced with a family breakfast. Mother insisted on this, said it was the time of day she set aside for us, her children – though I could never see that we were of much importance. Far too often there were guests who took her attention, or her husband of that period (she went through rather a lot of husbands in her day), and the talk was adult talk calculated to make children foreign. Angela always did her best to please in that anxious, compliant way she had which infuriated me. She dressed nicely, listened attentively, replied respectfully (if perhaps too avidly) when spoken to; whereas I, the bad child, I came into breakfast looking like a witch's apprentice with my hair unbrushed and unplaited, wearing dirty jodhpurs and a shirt which was too small for growing breasts. I would crash down in my place at the table, glower at all those present and then reach out a grubby hand for the best piece of pawpaw before Hassan came to pass it round. Bad manners were my pride and joy, my only security, my crowning achievement; Mother never once showed that she noticed.

I would much rather have stayed in bed. Beneath my bed-cover of Colobus monkey skins, sipping the tea Hassan would bring round while it was still dark, I felt like an animal secure in its burrow. I imagined myself to be something small like the hyraxes which shrieked all night in the forest (though out of bed and in daylight I felt like a vicious young civet cat) and I gathered up close to me whichever pet was allowed in my room at the time; maybe one of the dogs, or some creature I had found abandoned or wounded – a reedbuck fawn or a mongoose perhaps; I loved animals, would talk to them and knew they listened far more keenly than humans with their clever tricks of deafness. I wrote stories about my animals and recorded their daily experiences more fully than my own; I yearned to know what it was to be them, to see through their eyes. What did they think, what did they see and smell which we did not? Pets were my family, not Mother and Angela.

So I sat there at breakfast in hostile silence, loathing the guests and the sound of Angela's poor silly voice rushing forward then stumbling badly over consonants. On the few occasions when we had Mother to ourselves, Angela became unstoppable, gabbling incessantly her huge anxiety to please. She could never quite get it out, what she wanted to say, which was that she adored Mother and would have laid down her life to win the slightest sign of approbation.

But Mother herself needed encouragement from no one, so did not give it. Once she had put down her binoculars – and we had to wait in attendance for her attention – she presided over us looking as cool as the morning with her white skin and brilliant blue eyes, black hair a sleek bundle on her neck. She would cross her legs, light a cigarette, look away and hold us with her perfect poise. I see her now – bright colours always, her daytime shirts and scarves, and it strikes me as strange that someone so reserved and self-contained should authorize such reds and greens, sea blues to draw the eye. I can only conclude that they meant what they said: look at me, look again; I am not, or have not always been, precisely what I seem. Had she been less immaculate, less glacial, Mother might well have passed for a Bohemian. As it was her only artistic outlet was the piano (dragged up to Njoro by oxcart) which she played with cold passion and moderate technical skill. It was she who saw to it that I was taught to play, and I have always had a piano ever since, though the old Steinway here, which was hers, is badly out of tune and overrun with ants.

She liked to talk at breakfast about her current agricultural project.

'I have all the leaflets about Angora goats. Splendid animals, pleasant to tend, and rather a good investment, I should say. The climate here ought to be ideal, it's just a question of diseases, I expect, or some aspect of diet – it's always the little problems one least expects which cause difficulty. Still, I should love to try. Such beautiful creatures, you know.'

Mother was keen on animal husbandry though many of her projects ended in failure. Married to a 'verandah' farmer, she herself was never quite so supine and took a natural interest in the workings of the farm. An interest which Angela shared.

'Oh, M-Mummy, how perfectly marvellous. Mrs Holroyd has d-d-done awfully well with Angora rabbits.'

'Hardly the same thing, darling. What do you say, Hermione? Should we try goats?'

'I couldn't care less and I can't think why you ask – you'll do what you want to do anyway.'

Angela never failed to look aghast and personally wounded by my rudeness. 'Oh, H-H-Hermione, how c-can you say such a thing?' She remonstrated on Mother's behalf; I would retaliate with some practical gesture like eating the last piece of mango brought up from the coast, or dropping a brown furry caterpillar into her glass of passion fruit juice.

All of which Mother seemed not to notice. Averted, drawing deeply on her cigarette, she would gaze from the verandah down into the deep blue valley below where the lake gathered daylight as a pale pink definition of its shores; then upwards, up the hills on the other side and into the mountains beyond. Mother seemed to travel with her eyes so that while with us she was always elsewhere – alone on the rim of Menengai

53

Crater or scaling the ice-capped summit of Mount Kenya on clear days.

Mother's anger, the converse of her remoteness, was a swift igniting of the atmosphere which tended to occur when I least expected it; when I thought all likelihood of retribution had passed. From being nowhere, far out of reach, suddenly she was all around me, enveloping me in the flames of her insanity.

Strictly speaking I had earned her wrath each time, in one way or another, though never to that extent. Which was another thing about her anger – it was not proportional to the crime; it seemed to aim at deeper sins, the hidden ones which were quite unforgivable and might never be expunged. I could not predict when she would strike; again and again she would not notice my transgressions – then, without warning, an eruption, the ice barrier between us became a raging inferno – and not specifically because of what I had done but simply because her loathing had become unbearable. She would freeze away from me in dislike until the process cracked her, blew her wide open.

I remember the time I broke my arm while out shooting. Following the dark edge of the forest I had gone with my rifle to find reedbuck, dik-dik or bushbuck come out to dry their dappled coats in the late sunshine following the afternoon's heavy rains. I was climbing along the edge of a gulley, all red mud where the rain had eaten at it, when a flock of small birds startled me – they had nests in the gulley's cliff edges – and looking up to check their species (an ingrained habit, learned from Mother) I slipped over the edge, tumbled down and landed on rocks in a shallow torrent of muddy water.

Though my injured arm was very painful I took deep, passionate pride in hiding the fact from Mother. I was excluding her as she excluded me, and, I suppose, in this very way attracting her attention. I imagined dreadful wounds developing, sores worse than yaws; then maggots inhabiting the sores and other parasites like mango-fly larvae all living there in abundance so that, when Mother finally viewed my suffering, her horror would be so tremendous and her remorse (it was, after all, her fault) that . . . That what? That she would embrace me?

Her reaction was far from loving when she did find out, which was not long afterwards; Hassan knocked my arm as he was pouring sherry into the soup of my neighbour at the table – a Dr English, staying overnight – and I cried out involuntarily.

My secret revealed, Mother reacted contemptuously. 'Oh for heaven's sake, what did you hope to achieve by saying nothing? Foolish child.'

Dr English set my arm though Mother could have done it herself. She was highly experienced at treating minor injuries and diseases among servants, indeed, a patient and inquisitive nurse; but me she would not touch.

Later she visited me in my room when I was nearly asleep and assumed the incident closed.

Of course, in a curious way I coveted these scenes; they were the equivalent of loving exchanges between normal mothers and daughters. Our time of intimacy. Yet no one can tell me I did not suffer grievously: adult and mysterious anger is as terrifying to a child as any Greek deity's tantrums to the ancients.

I had been reading D. H. Lawrence in bed; Mother's copy of *Women in Love* taken from her office without asking. She grabbed it from my bedside table and hurled it across the room. The noise of its violent progress woke me to a wild-haired figure leaning over my pillow; a Gorgon, a Medusa, a Fury. I opened my eyes slowly in the hope that dread might banish her before I was fully awake.

Her face was undone, incoherent. 'You wanted me to suffer. You did it quite deliberately to show you have no trust, no faith. You would let yourself die as a torture, a hideous, endless torment. You wanted to deny me as your mother. In public.'

It was not so much the things she said as how she said them, with infinite contempt and abhorrence. That ripped right through me, no matter how I held myself aloof; which was my only tactic of defence, to become totally remote and distant, frozen hard into indifference – a reversal of roles, one might say. With resolutely empty eyes I looked up at bits of red moving in blackness – red mouth, red nails, red necklace, she was wearing her coral. Her eyes burning down saw more crime in me than I would ever have time to commit.

Raw and shrill, her voice went on and on. 'Why, Hermione, must you do this? Always. You, of all children. You have always rejected me. I should be used to it and yet each time it kills me. Why must you do this to me? Ironical, isn't it, that there can be children who bring not one ounce of joy. I wish that you would kill me, Hermione, instead of hurting me the way you do. The refusal to love – there is no pain worse than that. Why won't you love me?'

It was when her tirade touched on love that I knew she was no longer with me. I could hear some unbearable, dreadful frustration which had nothing to do with me – her words pierced my heart then passed on to their ultimate destination which was some other person or some place I'd never been. So that, in the end, our only kind of contact was not intimacy at all. The shock of this was always profound, and each time unexpected. I was alone, again left alone, and the terror this evoked expressed itself in the same worn words.

Each time I would say, 'I hate you' or 'I will never forgive you' or both.

And Mother would reply, 'It is all your fault. You are just like him.'

I only queried the 'him' later when I wrote such scenes into my diary. I presumed he must be my father.

Mother, for her part, was finished by the time she said 'him'. Scene over until the next time, she limped from my room like the shadow of a leopard leaving battle. But emotional violence took its toll. The next day she looked unslept, eyes haunted by dark circles, hair pulled back a bit too tightly.

I remember that I was allowed breakfast in bed on account of my broken arm. It was something special, freshly baked scones and blackberries Mother had harvested from some bushes which were producing their first crop of fruit. Angela came in to sit on the end of my bed.

'Isn't Mummy so kind? L-look what she had *mpishi* make for you.'

'For heaven's sake, Angela, you're squashing my feet. Typical, isn't it? You have the scones. I'm not hungry.'

Angela was speechless with anger in defence of Mother's breakfast tray. Then managed to trot out, 'You are n-not at all n-n-nice, Hermione. You are s-spoilt, that's all. Mummy spoils you and you d-don't even realize how lucky you are.'

'These berries are perfectly frightful. The *dudus* have got them. Here, catch.' And I tossed a small beetle at her which took to its wings almost instantly but not before she shrieked and leapt from the bed. Ever since I threw a grass snake at her (cruel, I admit, to the snake) she never waited to find out what was coming towards her. No sense of humour, Angela, nor reasonable backbone.

When I was not at school in Nairobi, I studied at home by correspondence course. Mother seemed to place more importance on my education than on Angela's, and about one thing she was most insistent – I must develop the art of writing well, she said, though I could never see why she took the thing so seriously. Poetry was another idea of hers; she forced my hand at it, and in the end the habit stuck for a lifetime.

Whatever Mother wanted I resisted, so the art of writing was one I came to secretly, in my own way. What I mean is, the essays and sonnets Mother made me write I deliberately sabotaged, ruined, rendered absurd and irrational; whereas my private writing - diaries, animal stories, free verse – was a way of speaking out when I had no one to speak to; they were my true thoughts and visions, my attempts to see order in the world. They kept me alive, and I kept them for years and years (until I left Montana). Everything Mother made me write I destroyed – and usually in front of her for maximum effect. During the rainy season when our fireplace was in use every evening, I heaved in the hated pages and watched their demise attract moths. At other times I was quite adept at shredding, or making cut-outs from the written pages as a mocking game, as proof of my resistance.

Angela, who never read or wrote a thing, spent much more time with Mother than I did. Together they supervised the tending of maize, checked on the chickens and ducks, the Angora goats, and discussed and planned new crops of veg-etables – was there a market for asparagus, would delphiniums do well in highland soil? Not that Mother listened to Angela; she was only a sounding board, it was hardly genuine dis-cussion; yet in a manner of speaking they shared the life of the farm. Which was also the life of the Kikuyu community who provided us with labour, and neighbours, none of them close by, with whom they exchanged visits or met at the crude little club in Njoro (nothing as grand as the Muthaiga). I shared in little of this, and told myself I had no wish to be included.

Outside agriculture, Mother's interests were all to do with escaping the earth; earthly ties, earthly duties. Apart from birdwatching, she collected butterflies. Her office was lined with glass cases behind which hovered beautiful and lifeless wings. Her own? I did wonder why she loved flying airplanes. It was fashionable, of course, for those who could afford it, and a convenient means of transport where roads were few, non-existent, or impassable during the rains. She was taught to fly by my father, her first husband, who had the time and money for such hobbies; divorced and married to poorer men, she nonetheless continued her hobby at any free opportunity offered her by friends. I seem to recall that once or twice she was even paid to fly from Nairobi, taking some small cargo further inland, or a visitor out to join a safari – all of which, I suppose, is testimony to her proficiency as a pilot. I imagined her alone in the cold still air above cloud, like an eagle circling Mount Kenya; such splendid isolation seemed her natural environment – it was the colour of her eyes, I thought, which matched the sky at icy altitudes.

Mother was as cool and efficient at managing her social life as she was with everything else. Her fourth husband, Major Weaver, known as Jock to his friends, was fond of 'cutting a dash' in Nairobi at the seasonal races or the Muthaiga Club, and accepted any invitation he could get to drunken houseparties in the 'aristocratic' Aberdares. I see nothing when I think of him, just a tall thin outline curved in jocularity; perhaps a small moustache. Mother did him proud as a consort. With her impeccable looks and natural elegance, she managed always to look chic and fashionable, with hats, silk dresses, strings of pearls which were once her mother's. Properly attired she knew how to stand, never let her body go – or, if she slouched, she did so to good effect. She was more aristocratic in her looks than many of the titled people with whom she and Jock socialized, and I felt that she believed herself superior to them – one of nature's élite, just as the Masai were noble savages among lesser primitives. (Mother was no democrat but unpredictably snobbish: she deplored Lady Delamere's 'bad blood' – whatever that was – but approved of the infamous American, Alice de Trafford.)

Looks were only part of Mother's social success; the other aspect was frosty charm: a certain cold-blooded interest she would turn on people like the hypnotic gaze of a snake. And they were mesmerized. They thought her perceptive and entertaining, and I suppose she had a certain virtuosity in caustic comments and sardonic observation. She knew how to flatter, where necessary, and how to cut dead the 'wrong' people – I've seen her do it to perfection. I detested her social behaviour and mannerisms; and yet she was sought-after company, her house was a popular stop-over for friends from Nairobi heading inland. So was there something I missed? Some glimmer of warmth which escaped me and fled to outsiders?

I hated to watch Mother surrounded by friends.

'She adores admiration. God knows why, it's all so shallow,' I said to Angela.

'Mummy doesn't r-really enjoy herself, you know. She d-does it for Jock.'

'For him? You are silly, Angela. When has Mother ever done anything for anyone but herself? She's an egoist, she's totally self-centred.'

'You are the egoist, H-Hermione. And you're jealous. Yes, j-jealous. You simply can't bear sharing Mummy with other people, you w-want her all to yourself, despite the f-fact that you're always so m-mean to her.'

'At least I don't bore her like you do.'

It was so easy getting in the last word. Angela's three years' head start on me brought her no advantages. There she was, a large-boned, well-developed woman (alien stock, different from Mother and me), while I, a scrawny, pre-pubescent creature, held her dignity to ransom without effort.

Another reason why I hated to see Mother in full social swing was the way some men looked at her: with obscure and furtive yearning, always of the most intense kind, this secret coveting which seemed a cruel mimicry of my own, and sharp rivalry. Were their chances any better than mine?

I suspected Mother. I was sure that one or more of her male admirers had assumed my rightful place in her heart. I knew, somehow I was certain, that Mother was in love, she felt a hard and icy passion towards someone. That is, I felt this to be true, though I would still have said, if asked, that Mother loved no one but herself. (Certainly she did not love her husband.) There was never any evidence of an extra-marital liaison, but that was inconsequential; like a sensitive spouse I sensed infidelity instinctively – though my instincts with regard to Mother were both acute and wildly distorted. On the basis of novels I was reading at the time about promiscuous adult life, I assumed that my rival was probably more than one person, or a sequence of men, and this assumption dulled a little the huge throbbing of rage and resentment which such considerings caused me.

I tried out my suspicions on Angela. 'Mother has a lover,' I said in a casual way one morning after breakfast. The air was crisp with the fresh smell of dew and juniper, but Angela looked like a wilted overblown flower – she was interested in men; had stayed up far too late entertaining, unchaperoned, a young district officer passing through. The evening, I supposed, had not been a success. 'Mother has a lover,' I repeated, with the emphasis now on 'Mother' who did, while Angela did not.

'Don't be ridiculous.' At first she forgot to stammer in her genuine indignation. 'Mummy is not like that. W-what an awful thing to say. You are so spiteful and m-malicious, Hermione. Sometimes I don't think you can r-really be my s-s-sister at all. Poor M-Mummy must have got the wrong baby.'

'Dr English would have had to be awfully quick to switch me. But perhaps he didn't need to be – perhaps I was already somebody else's. Different father, I mean: one of Mother's lovers.'

'You are a w-witch, Hermione. Wicked, just wicked.' She was very angry indeed, but I thought her description of me rather interesting and original. I liked it: a witch. I felt like one, all dark and separate; if only I were one it would explain everything – and give me powers over Mother.

When Angela was soon to leave us to be married and sail for England, I decided that I must go as well. This decision came upon me suddenly when I realized one morning that, in the near future, there would only be the two of us at breakfast (when there were no guests, of course). The two of us: that state of affairs to which I secretly aspired. Was it finally to be my reward for years of patient resentment, persistent hostility? I was finely balanced between huge expectation – maybe this time, maybe finally – and black pessimism: she had failed me before, she would fail me again. In the end it was cunning which won out; I reasoned that the 'two of us' would happen if I left. Losing me would fix my image in her mind as obsessively as hers was forever in mine. I would leave, never return, never write (and I stuck by my resolution, not even one letter between us), and the silence would speak and the empty place at the table until I was a constant voice, an incessant companion, because the tension between us had never been resolved.

In a way, I suppose, I must have cherished the way things were; I was used to our distances only broken by wild and terrible rows. I was used to my prison, so to speak, and left it in order that the terms of imprisonment might continue indefinitely. I must have suspected that perhaps, finally, relations might begin to improve between Mother and me; and I did not want a pleasant, placid home (not ever a strong likelihood). But there was more to it than that. I believe that I actually feared what I most desired: the idea of an embrace, of hard attachment which I so badly wanted on the day my father left, I could not bear as a possible reality. And why? Because reality can never match fantasy? Because the intensity I yearned for could never be sustained? I simply cannot read myself from that angle, even now. Mysteries remain, always mysteries.

I had realized that I was not the only person to wonder about Mother and men. Wives did, the wives of men who came to visit too frequently. And I began to contrive my escape by making use of the jealousy of one particular wife, a Mrs Peak, whose husband came often to the farm to consult with Mother on this and that matter, just excuses, about maize and the marketing of it. I told Mrs Peak that I thought it was 'just excuses' which brought him, and the way her face twisted over with malice made me respect her. I talked to her about Angela's forthcoming marriage, and how I too dreamed of living in London one day. As soon as possible. I added that it would 'break Mother's heart' to lose both her daughters simultaneously.

And that did it: Mrs Peak made enquiries, pulled strings, and found a family which needed a companion for their children during the voyage back to England. The governess appointed was too ill to travel; I might take her place. 'They were concerned about your age,' said Mrs Peak, 'but I assured them that you are very mature for sixteen.' At which she had to look away from my delinquent child stare; I disturbed her.

The night before I left, Mother played the piano for longer than usual as if she could not bear to stop. It was a cold and damp evening, the fire was burning, we were alone – no guests, Jock away on safari. The thought occurred to me that she was missing Angela. They had often played duets together, and sometimes when I watched them closely I could see in the way they laughed together, the way their eyes met, something I could not understand at all. As if I knew nothing about their real feelings for each other, or what they were in themselves. And then, like a glimpse down an endless dark tunnel, I would sense, falling backwards, the existence of a simultaneous but different version of events, an alternative narrative I could neither read nor destroy. What did I really know? How greatly might I be wrong?

I knew it was not wrong to suppose that if Mother missed Angela the loss of me would be a crushing blow.

I had not told her yet – I was leaving the next day and still I had not told her. It was my intention to leave a note behind the way suicides do, so to maximize the pain of loss without face-to-face farewell. Yet when I heard her play on and on, Chopin, Brahms, Beethoven, and the saddest pieces she could find, I thought with an animal's precision of instinct: she is weak now, strike immediately.

'I am leaving tomorrow,' I said in a casual way.

She looked up from the piano and her hands, heavy with rings and bracelets, dropped automatically into her lap. 'I know.'

Plain, unembroidered words without expression. No remonstrations, no exhortations to stay; no regrets. She knew – heaven knows how – and she accepted my decision as though she had no right to stop me; or no such desire. She was wearing a green dress and the red coral necklace, and her hair rested like a gleaming pelt on the back of her neck. How well I knew her, every inch of her body, each movement; incompatible she and I might be, but we were the same person, the same flesh. Yet she would not keep me – no tears, no pleading. Without a moment's hesitation she left me to my self-designed fate.

I hate you: but this time I would not say it.

She was the one with words; she said 'I know' again and it seemed to be the first time she had ever spoken to me. There was more I must know. 'Hermione, you will have to come back. Some day. For your sake and for mine. It would not be right to leave things as they are for ever. One day you will come home again.'

Her hands were so tightly entwined with each other that the knuckles were white, her rings mortified the flesh. I was intrigued by the way they could hurt each other so much, those two hands, even though they came from the same body and felt the same pain.

SIX

❧❧❧❧❧❧❧❧❧❧❧❧❧❧❧❧❧❧

Nicola had trouble opening her front door and, though I thought at first that it must be the lock, I could see when she finally succeeded that her hands were shaking. For some reason she lacked self-control.

'Do come . . .' Before entering she raised her face to the wintery sky and gulped in air like a fish at the surface of a pond.

It was part of a terrace which backed onto the river. Georgian, Nicola said, but most popular at the turn of the century when fashionable artists colonized the area. This particular house had been owned before Augustus by his great-aunt, who had been a member of the Royal Academy and well known for her gentle watercolours of the riverside.

'Have I told you how Augustus got . . . his great-aunt insisted on the name, you see, because she had known him, Augustus John, I mean, and admired his work greatly, so that . . .' Nicola was sifting through mail which had fallen through the letter box.

'Rather a mouthful for a child, to be called Augustus.'

'His friends call him Gus but . . .'

'But you don't.'

She looked at me steadily for a moment, then wafted away. She had draped her cloak across the banister where it lay like a black shroud, like the empty shadow of someone recently dead. As she moved down the narrow corridor towards light from the dining room she ran her fingers through her hair, dislodging large strands from the braid, and shivered a trembling motion down her entire body so that the mauve chiffon skirt she was wearing, a sadly inadequate garment, caught on her black lace-up boots. The tiny sounds of damage which ensued did not seem to reach her.

I followed her into the kitchen, which had shocked me when I first saw it on my last visit. The counter was stained and chipped, no cupboards, just grubby, open shelves; the stove was an ancient gas-ringed affair and the fridge like an icebox from way back in the 'thirties. Though small, the kitchen might have been workable had Nicola kept it tidy; instead it was littered chaotically with pots and pans containing leftovers, glass jars filled with shrivelled herbs and spices, odd vegetables strayed from the rest of their kind, and miscellanea: a remarkable assortment of vitamin pills, old bills, concert notices, and bits and pieces of ethnic jewellery which Nicola had no doubt removed whilst cooking and forgotten for ever. I thought it quite remarkable that she managed to produce meals at all in such an environment.

Now she was producing tea. After filling an ancient and battered kettle with water, she placed it on a gas ring and lit a match. Looking away vaguely into the inner reaches of the house, nose up, eyes violet in the gloom, she reached out with it hopefully, and in the whoosh of flame which announced success the sleeve of her blouse – something peasanty and embroidered – caught fire. Nicola, I gasped and darted forward. She glanced around with mild disinterest.

'Oh yes, all the time . . . but then it's hardly surprising considering . . . and then again I am a fire sign, odd, isn't it, but so was Matty.'

She ran her wrist under the cold tap and the smell of spoiled fire was unpleasant, petty, rather chemical like kerosene; the material of her sleeve was a synthetic despite its rural pretensions.

We sat in the upstairs sitting room for tea, by the floor-to-ceiling windows with warped glass which overlooked the river. The day had greyed as it drew towards premature night, and

66

a few streaks of pearly pink showed in the west already at three in the afternoon. The river looked like mercury, thick and sluggish, yet the flotsam and jetsam of the city rushed past rapidly towards the sea.

'Does anything live in it?' I asked, of the river.

'They do say that . . . a few fish and swans, reappearing, but nobody swims, unless they have to, I mean all those rowing sculls, some must capsize if . . .'

'It reminds me of the Ganges. A place to sprinkle the ashes of dead relatives.'

'One lump or two? or perhaps . . .' Nicola's head dipped over the tea tray. I noticed a few grey hairs, secret memento mori; already? at thirty-five? Mother hadn't a single one when I left home – and she must have been forty then.

'None. Just milk. When is Augustus due home?'

'Well, it's hard to . . . especially now, at Christmas, with the suicides, it's the season, you know.'

'I should have thought it was the season of goodwill and festivity. But still.'

'That's just it, you see, people . . . it's the feeling left out of it all, pain does that, you know, and then seeing others so together makes the isolation seem much worse but . . .'

Nicola's hand was shaking again and she spilled my tea; drew out a used Kleenex from her damp sleeve and tried to wipe up. But there were noises downstairs, her head shot up, she forgot what she was doing. (I reached over and took the cup for myself, topped it up from the pot.)

'Augustus?' I asked.

She nodded, and while I watched her long face underwent an abrupt transformation from pure crystal joy to heavy reluctance; as though she had changed her mind about Augustus in mid-thought. Or suddenly remembered something she had been trying to forget. After a moment's pause, too long, she called out to him: 'Darling, we're . . . bring a cup, and perhaps . . .'

*

He did not mount the stairs quietly; awaiting him, one expected a huge, bumbling animal to burst through the doorway. Instead, revealed, he was rather a small man, though a little fat, and his excessive clumsiness, which accounted for the bangings and shufflings en route, derived from permanent preoccupation with his profession: he never stopped thinking about patients and the healing of them. He had a hygienic beard and a rather blotchy skin, and small unshielded eyes which seemed to be searching for spectacles. When he spoke it was the voice of the consulting room, artificially mellowed, confidential, almost whispering; yet ringing with absolute, unyielding authority backed up by an upper-class accent which was rather too royal to be true. It seemed to me that he would have liked to be God; the medical profession was only second best but near enough to satisfy his enormous hunger for power. Over lives, the little lives of others.

Those were my impressions collected when I first met Augustus. I disliked him on sight, automatically. This in no way distressed me or proved an embarrassment; it was only to be expected that if I were drawn to Nicola I would find her husband repellent. My antipathy towards him was proof of my loyalty and affection for her.

I recalled what in particular had finished Augustus with me. He had expounded, at length and minutes after meeting me, his philosophy of medicine which dignified itself with the rather pretentious title of Holism. What did this mean? His explanation left me only a little wiser yet disturbed. For he was talking about the 'whole person' as the preserve of the doctor, his professional playground extended from bodies to minds and souls too. The lot. This alarmed me, I felt keen repugnance: they want complete control, I thought, will these doctors leave nothing alone? Imagine how infuriating to visit some general practitioner with a sore finger and be asked about potty training or one's notion of the ever-after – none of anyone else's business, for heaven's sake. Stick to stomachs (his specialization): I said this to Augustus, made my indignation clear. Because I knew he wanted everything from everyone, just as much as he could winkle out and swallow – and his appetite was voracious.

'Super, how marvellous to see you again, Hermione.' His doctor's soft hands were upon me, patting my shoulders. (The importance of touching – that was one of his dictums and another infringement on privacy.)

'You're home early, Augustus.' I drew back.

'Super, absolutely super.'

And then he ambled like a bear over to Nicola, kissed the top of her head. 'By the way, darling, have you seen that article on *myocardial ischaemia* I was reading yesterday?'

She looked both startled and vague, which meant she was mentally searching. 'It seems to me that . . .' He dropped down heavily into an armchair and she poured him some tea but without paying attention to the task at hand; long nose delicately searching the air, hovering over various possible hiding places, she was still thinking about the missing article.

Looking at Augustus sipping tea it struck me how much the house resembled him, or vice versa, rather as people come to look like their pets. The tweedy confidence of his stout figure matched perfectly the solidity of the patched leather armchairs and settee; the huge, dark Victorian sideboard and bookcases were as dominating and oppressive as his ideas. Which ruled: everywhere there were piles of medical texts, dissertations, collections of conference papers, clinical data, work-in-progress reports; but no art books. No evidence of Nicola. And the medical bric-a-brac, amusing antiques such as wooden heads painted with surgical diagrams, old trusses, Victorian artificial limbs, these had certainly not been chosen by Nicola. It was almost as if she did not live here.

Where did she work, I wondered? Surely she had space of her own, somewhere to do her illustrations. He must allow her that.

I said to him, 'I see you have a lot of your great-aunt's watercolours about. Why nothing of your wife's?'

He was only half paying attention; his eyes were scanning the room for the paper he wanted. 'Lovely, aren't they, Bessie's little pictures. Worth quite a bit these days too.'

'Had a good day, darling? I did wonder if . . .' murmured Nicola inconclusively. She was not drinking her own tea; took one sip, I noticed, then put it down with distaste.

'A frustrating day, darling. One of my cancer patients refused further treatment. She said she simply wanted to be left in peace. I tried to explain that it will hardly be peaceful for her once she can no longer eat properly and the pain increases. However, she was adamant. Sometimes I think doctors ought to have the power to make decisions for patients who can obviously not judge for themselves. It is wrong to give in to disease.'

'"Do not go gentle into that good night",' I quoted ironically.

'But you know, darling, there are people who . . . you see, fighting is not for everyone, sometimes peace is what . . . especially in cases of terminal disease.'

Nicola's face looked strained like a stutterer's, she seemed to be struggling with the limitations of her style of speech. Something very important was trying to get out; yet remained contained because, ultimately, it was not her way to reveal herself. I was puzzled and intrigued. If nothing else I heard dissension between husband and wife. Last time Nicola had been totally in agreement with Augustus, on everything. So what had changed?

He was also surprised and came back at her almost gruffly. 'There is no such thing as terminal disease. Once you admit that all of medicine will vanish. It is only by refusing to accept death that its powers are diminished, that we push back the frontiers of mortality. One day everyone will live for ever.'

'Perish the thought.' Really, the man was too much. 'I for one shall most definitely not let some snotty-nosed young doctor keep me alive beyond a good life. Cruel, is what I call the artificial sustaining of things. Nothing to do with compassion, all this forcing of a miserable existence on people who would rather die. But still.' I leaned back in my chair and gave him a long sideways look.

He returned it with a gaze of surgical precision. 'I cannot imagine, Hermione, that anyone could ever force anything on you.'

Then he gulped back the dregs of his tea and got up. 'Must work,' he said. 'I have a paper to finish for New Year.'

As he passed Nicola on his way out his hand hovered briefly over her head like a saint dispensing miracles, and he turned to me and said, 'She is beautiful, isn't she? The most beautiful woman in the world.' Saying this, all at once he was different, as if love undid him, and he was young and raw and supplicant before this woman who was his wife and his life – for it seemed that all he had made of himself depended on her approval. Eyelids at half-mast, she smiled her half-smile. And he relaxed, once more certain that his existence was justified. It seemed to me a ritual I had witnessed. His hand above her was the hand of healing and when she smiled she accepted his cure, and was healed. To do otherwise would have destroyed him.

But Nicola's hands in her lap were clenched, white at the knuckles, the delicate length of her artist's fingers stretched to breaking point. Mother's hands, I thought; Mother's hands like that meant pain, too much tension, something quite unbearable. But what? The marriage seemed what is technically referred to as 'stable'; nonetheless I felt that in some way as yet hidden, perhaps only dimly perceived by those concerned, Nicola was leaving Augustus. Or beginning to prepare for a departure. And I was glad.

I was glad, and unashamed to be so. After all, it was Nicola I had come to see, she was family and husbands are not. I felt slightly triumphant as if I were about to lose a rival. Nicola was more mine than his, my rights to her were stronger, my needs more legitimate.

As though shaking herself free from my thoughts Nicola suddenly pointed out the window. (Bracelets jangled, earrings tinkled.) 'Look, Hermione, a pair of ringed wood-pigeons in the oak tree, they often come into the . . . last winter I left bread in the garden but the gulls got it, and then there was the blue jay too, most lovely.'

It was dark. We were alone and able to talk. When Nicola switched on a light, it was our light, there to illuminate private matters concerning no one else but the two of us.

I said to her, 'Did Mother tell you much about herself?'

'I would say she told me everything there was to . . . and later her letters, well, she wrote so well, like you, Hermione, you are so like her.'

'I would like to know more about Mother. And now that she is dead there is no one but you to help me in this. You see, I'd like a fuller picture – don't ask me why.'

My nonchalance was assumed: suddenly the need to know was a huge pressure on my selective memory which faltered when I looked at Nicola who had loved Mother, and who, for that reason, reminded me of those panic-stricken moments of doubt when I watched Mother and Angela at the piano play out their secret version of family relatedness which had nothing whatsoever to do with mine.

'Knowledge is freedom, but surely you know as much as I . . .'

'Oh, I know the basics, darling, but not much in the way of details. You see, Mother and I never talked. Angela used to pass things on but I never trusted her versions of events. Muddle-headed, I'm afraid, was old Angela.'

'Poor Mummy, she . . . never knew everything.'

'But you and I can discuss it all.' Nicola said nothing so I added, 'Tell me about your visits to Mother when you were a child.'

SEVEN

❧❧❧❧❧❧❧❧❧❧❧❧❧❧❧❧❧

After Mother's fourth husband died, she sold the farm at Njoro and moved to Dar es Salaam. Friends had suggested Mombasa if it was a change of climate she was after, but there was more she wanted – a sense of starting anew in another country. Perhaps at the age of fifty she felt the last stirrings of youth in her and wanted to make a new beginning while she still might; but certainly when Angela wrote to me about Mother's move I found it odd, felt there must be other reasons.

She bought a plot of land just outside of Dar es Salaam along the beach and had a bungalow built there.

'Just like the one in south India where she was . . . Matty always said that the first house in one's life is the best and it's where one always wants to return to, well, in her case she couldn't go back to where she lived as a child but at least she was on the Indian Ocean in a bungalow modelled on . . .'

For several summers in sequence Nicola travelled out to stay with Mother; at that time a difficult journey for a child of eight or so, involving several changes of plane. As Angela lacked the wherewithal, Mother must have paid for the plane fares – though where she found the cash was a mystery because I had never known her to have money of her own; there was always some man to support her.

'Just being together, well, it's hard to . . . we loved each other's company, you know, every minute of it, and I've never known such pleasure in companionship since, though, of course, it's only natural . . .'

Such statements jettisoned all reason: who was I, and who was this woman she adored? The panic I felt was the risk of fact obliteration, or an inversion of truths, all the truths I had known. I felt as if, in discussing Mother, we were looking at an ambiguous object picture in which some see an old hag and some a lovely girl: we both of us knew Mother yet perceived two different individuals (and called her different names).

The qualities in Mother which made me hate her inspired Nicola to love her. The meaning, the significance, was different in her case. Mother's cold aloof manner meant capability and strength, the steely determination that nothing would affect her adversely and that, in consequence, she could be relied upon always and in all ways. Indomitable, her protection was absolute, unvarying – she provided a sense of security Nicola had never known before with her absentee father and invalid mother.

'With Matty I felt I could be a child, she didn't need me to take care of . . .'

Mother would never have let anyone take care of her – her self-reliance was tyrannical and unkind. Yet to Nicola it was something hopeful and meant that she too might stand alone, might be exactly who she chose to be with no help or assistance from others. There was something of that attitude, I thought, behind her unfocused mannerisms: a fixity, a precise definition of her own independence. Did Augustus know this or would it come as a shock?

Women like Mother have always made better grandparents than parents. The child of their child comes by way of companionship without responsibility and the dreary repetitions of daily life. Nicola was a guest – and Mother always adored having visitors, was at her best with admiring strangers around. I believe there is always a strong affinity between generations-once-removed, just as talents and defects tend to skip a generation. Mother and Nicola were likely to like each other, even likely to love, though not to the extent that they did.

Of course there was one thing missing. One aspect of Mother

which was central to my knowledge of her Nicola never so much as suspected. Her anger. So where was it? Had her life changed so much? I would like to think that rage, the raging rows which flared up between us, were strictly inherent to our relationship – and that no one but me ever made Mother feel quite so beside herself, so dreadfully unhinged. Hatred is as special as love.

And perhaps for this reason it did not occur to me to feel jealous of Nicola; she had taken nothing that was mine. Disbelieving, sceptical, I nonetheless strained to catch each word of care and admiration, I wanted to hear enough to feel their relationship. And I wanted it wonderful as if Nicola were me, taking my place in a substitute childhood. One can never be jealous of oneself.

Nicola described her temporary life with Mother by telling me about their daily routine; as if this were of the essence, what they did together each day, day after day. And I thought that for the old and young, yes, the quality of life is in its management, and quality is all, for what both realize is the message so forgotten in the middle years, that the purpose of life is living. Nothing more, nothing less.

'I so looked forward to breakfast, such a fresh time of day, and Matty at her best, just bursting with a kind of cool and contained enthusiasm for the day which I admired enormously . . . and the way she could control it, never let too much show like . . .'

'I dare say it helped that there was no one else there. No houseguests. The number of times your mother and I had her to ourselves could be counted on one hand. But still.'

'We weren't always alone, sometimes he . . . but then I never minded company.'

'And what about the birds? Mother used to spend half of breakfast looking at the wretched things through binoculars. Which was hardly conducive to intimacy.'

'Oh yes, the birds . . . they seemed exactly the right start to the day, something so free, I mean, and beautiful . . . I rather see her early morning birdwatching as akin to a pagan praying to the sun, in a way, though she was also a born naturalist, quite scientific really.'

Breakfast was just as formal as it had been in my day – Mother keeping up standards. Fruit served on silver platters, eggs in monogrammed eggcups, good porcelain teacups in which to enjoy the true flavour of upcountry tea, a beaded net to cover the milk jug, tongs for the sugar bowl (though no kitchen toto to pass it). There were always flowers, marigolds or bougainvillaea floating in a polished brass bowl, and properly starched napkins folded into defiant icebergs waiting out the heat for the next laundry. And if there had not been ritualistic trappings of civilization? Like all foreigners, Mother's life was held together by these bits of evidence of origin and status.

At the end of breakfast Mother would light her first cigarette of the day. (This was a departure from habit: in my day she started smoking immediately – at once the haze of smoke between us.) She had taken to using an ivory holder and her cigarettes were black, something deadly from Zanzibar. As she smoked, red lips parted, red nails flicking ash, she would turn sideways in her chair and look out to sea, pausing intermittently to sweep glances over her young companion. And all the while she talked, about birds, about the dhows out at sea, and about what the two of them would do together that day. Nicola was as fascinated by the way she looked as by the words which came out of her. The impeccable grooming, the perfect clothes: all further evidence of extreme self-control. A marvellous power over chaos.

'I thought her the most beautiful person, she was so striking and elegant, like you, Hermione, and . . . she didn't look her age at all, the way she walked, so slim, from behind she might have been in her twenties . . . especially with her hair down, you know, because it was still . . .'

'Still black? I dare say she dyed it. Mother always was frightfully vain.'

'And you . . . I mean, your hair is white, so you let it . . . ?'

'I have never let anything go, darling. Grey suits me.'

After breakfast Mother and Nicola would go for a walk along the beach. Mother took a large *kikapu* with her in which to carry back fish bought at the nearby fishing village. She would bargain for these with a keen sense of justice: she would not pay expatriate prices, always highly inflated, but neither did she expect, nor would accept, the very little which the villagers themselves paid for fish. She was in all this a memsahib and a foreigner, white African but not native African ('two-year wonders', the professionals who came out on contract, were the sort from whom she felt most distant). The villagers knew her well and respected her – referred to her as the *memsabu mkubwa* – though in one respect they found her quite incomprehensible, and that was her commissioning of young men from the village to catch live coral fish in jam jars.

Mother's agrarian interests had been supplanted by a passion for collecting fish. She had several large aquaria bought abroad somewhere by a friend, and into them she introduced a variety of small reef fish and live corals. A new hobby but not unlike her interest in birds, I thought, in that fish too are not of the earth.

'Matty made it wonderfully interesting, her fish, I mean . . . the way she described them . . . and she was so exact, so observant, because, as she put it, she would not like not to know all there was to . . .'

'Sounds like her dissertations about pet projects round the farm. She would bore me to death with details.'

'I was never bored, you see, because . . .'

Because of love.

But Nicola shook her head, she could see I had not finished her sentence entirely. 'Yes, that and . . . because she inspired me, I mean, her objectivity . . . to observe without self in the way, I try to do it now when I paint but . . . it was not something poor Mummy could teach.'

So the absence of emotion was a virtue; distance and impersonality a high achievement. When to me they were death, the slow killing of the spirit. I believed in passion, in rampant subjectivity – this time I shook my head. Yet Nicola and I could afford different viewpoints, we were meant to be polarized, and it was for this reason that I listened.

At midday, while the heat baked the sandy garden and blistered the tin roof, Mother and Nicola slept; around four they awoke to fresh lime juice brought by the houseboy. A second awakening, a second chance to enjoy the day.

If the tide was in they went swimming.

'Matty had a very beautiful black swimming costume, from France, she said, he brought it over, whereas I . . . something pink and ruffled Mummy bought but Matty was kind about it, she always said I looked like a flower floating just below the surface and . . .'

Occasionally Mother would swim far out alone and then float on her back like a drifting log until Nicola became anxious and called her. And then she swam back, immediately. (How many times did I silently call her and when did she ever come? Yet I know she was constantly aware – how else would she have managed to be so evasive?)

When fleets of tiny fishing boats skimmed past for the evening catch, they went back to the house for tea. Another formal ritual with porcelain and silverware. And the time of day when Mother liked to reminisce, and Nicola adored listening.

The past of a grandparent is always attractive; there is freedom to it absent from parental histories which hold dogmatic lessons, morals and fresh grief. But grandparents are distant enough in time from events they describe to let it be art –

amusing fiction, light fantasy. Which is how children see their own daily lives.

I imagined Nicola rapt with attention, listening hard for each detail with unqualified admiration which indicates an imagination full and active. The chemistry of empathy; I know nothing of it, yet Nicola confessed, 'I wished that I was . . . her, I mean, that I might grow up to be her.' Nicola actually said this.

Most of the stories about Mother's childhood in India were harmless, though sometimes a raw note was hit – but never a raw nerve; it was fiction, after all, oral storytelling, a form of entertainment.

'Matty told me once about her sister, quite a bit younger, I think, who . . . it was some sort of bonfire, and the little girl stretched out her white pinafore too close to the fire and . . . that was it, you see, a terrible tragedy, up in flames so quickly, and her hair was red too, the colour of fire . . . Matty said she used to wear green ribbons to show off her hair, so sad, and it affected her deeply, I . . .'

'I think, darling, you must be wrong. God knows, no one's memory is infallible, but I never ever heard anything about a sister who burned to death. Not even from Angela. And it's hardly the sort of story one forgets.'

'Quite possibly Mummy didn't . . . Matty might not have told her.'

And yet she told this child everything, transposed into her a lifetime of memory. Telling, I suppose, is a form of auto-biography undertaken for someone in particular. For me? Was Nicola a medium, like a book with my name on it, through which Mother was speaking to me?

Imagine, I thought, (for I could not imagine it) conversation with Mother instead of silences or rage. Mother not only told Nicola tales about herself but also listened to the child describe her own life back in London.

Indeed, Mother encouraged Nicola to talk about herself but always in the right way. 'If you do not put yourself in a flattering light, darling, no one else will,' was Mother's message.

And I wondered whether she attempted to remedy the child's delivery as well as content. Dropping words and phrases was the opposite of Angela's stammer which repeated sounds – yet both were abnormal, inelegant, not up to Mother's 'standards'. Perhaps at that age Nicola had been even less coherent and heavily handicapped by the eager paralysis of the child who is never listened to trying to get too much out. 'Mummy never had time to . . . her attention was gone before I had finished.' So why bother to finish at all?

But Mother wanted all the endings and gave them ample time to arrive. She encouraged Nicola to talk about things which could never be discussed with Angela. Like her father: how often was he drunk, what happened, how did Angela react? And Nicola herself: how did she feel, was she frightened, was she angry? 'There is no one but me you can tell this to,' said Mother. 'You must never discuss family outside of family. So tell me all, darling. The worst is to keep silent.' Was she thinking of me and my silences?

'Sometimes I became . . . overwrought, because, you know, it was distressing to me really, and when I felt tears starting to come I would dash over to Matty and climb into her lap, wrap my arms around her tightly, and . . . I remember one evening we had been talking and I ran to her and knocked over the kerosene lamp which very nearly started a . . . but she was quick, she put out the flames.'

I could see them together and, in that act of seeing, experienced vicarious comfort. They loved each other with my hatred.

But was it too late, was it really too late? Mother was dead but here was Nicola, and might not she change sides, try Mother's role for my sake? Love is love, does it matter which part in it one takes? Mother had sent me Nicola when she could not come herself; I was elated by the notion and temporarily young within it.

My narrative, Nicola's narrative – opposite and yet the same if only I could find some point of intersection, perhaps a simple piece of information. Nicola would know.

As for Nicola, she sat and smiled at her story as the river outside turned black. She smiled like the child she had been at the time, full of optimism and the freshness of life itself. The way Mother used to make her feel she had made herself feel by remembering. In the feeble lamplight her skin took on a lustrous glow which affirmed the power of blood and memory to defy death, to deny even her own.

Then she put out her hand and touched me terribly lightly, more the brush of a cobweb than real human contact. I knew by this that she meant to draw me in, to weave me into her memories, just as I was weaving her into mine.

EIGHT

❧❧❧❧❧❧❧❧❧❧❧❧❧❧❧❧❧❧

It started to snow as we drove to the airport the next morning to pick up Susan.

Nicola was shivering as if she had never been warm. 'I just knew . . . when I woke up, you see, I had been dreaming about rain . . . but snow is different, I lack all resistance to cold these days which is hardly surprising considering that . . . but perhaps if I had slept better.'

'Not coming down with flu, are you, darling? How perfectly frightful that would be, with Christmas so close. Tell you what: when we get back, I'll make the tea and you pop off for a while – take up the prone position. Does one a power of good.'

Nicola blew her nose on a huge, man's handkerchief and shook her head. 'Oh no, really, not flu, and I prefer to keep busy, you see, because . . .'

Huge flakes suddenly besieged us, splattering against the windows of the taxi like white moths bent on destruction. Then, as suddenly as they had started, they stopped; and I felt the way I used to feel in Africa waiting for rain, when the necessary deluge failed or teased with a few ponderous droplets, then nothing. The atmosphere outside was thick, oppressive, while inside the taxi the air was too hot, and sweet with an odour issuing from Nicola, perhaps some health shop perfume of crushed flowers – but now their scent was one of decay, the stench of dying vegetation. I began to feel nauseous and opened the window a fraction. Nicola reacted with a terrible shudder and pulled further inside of her foolish black cloak which clung to her as if she might give it warmth.

'You know, darling, you really ought to have something a bit warmer. It's just the thing one does, dressing properly. The human race would never have survived if everyone went around as you do.'

'Yes, survive, which is why there's no point now in . . . and anyway I couldn't wear furs, they make me sad, I think of animals suffering though . . . I mean, they do suit you so well, Hermione, and with your jewellery and that wonderful watch . . .'

'Cartier.' (The name meant nothing to her.) 'Well, darling, if you won't change your dressing habits, then you'd better change where you live. By the way, what's happening to Mother's bungalow by the beach? Now there's an ideal getaway in a hot climate – not bad for an artist, I dare say.'

Nicola stopped trembling and seemed unnaturally still as if she might have stopped breathing as well. Automatically alarmed I glanced round. Her nose was brittle, her mouth strained and white, and I wondered for a moment: was she angry? But I knew that was impossible, anger was not part of her vague vocabulary; so perhaps she was feeling whatever caused anger, like loneliness, isolation, fear. Afraid? Surely not that – she had me.

'I believe, or so Kumar told me, that your mother left her house to . . .'

'To you. Congratulations. Now all you have to do is give up everything – illustrating, way of life, husband – and you can go and enjoy it.'

'Yes.'

I had never before heard her give a one-word reply. But when I checked she was pulling on fingerless gloves (not much warmth to be had there) so I assumed she was not listening or had forgotten to finish.

When we arrived at the airport terminal we discovered that Susan's plane was delayed by half an hour.

'Typical. She's never been on time for anything in her life. Not even her wedding.'

Nicola murmured something incoherent which I took to indicate sympathetic interest. She was smoking, eyes dreamy as though inhaling lovely, distant visions with each mouthful of grey fumes. When we sat down to wait on some spotted chairs her head fell backwards at such an angle to her neck that it looked like a flower just snapped from its stalk in an exaggerated version of Mother's favourite mannerism. How she had copied her, I thought, and yet remained unique. This reflection both depressed and encouraged me.

'Have I told you about Susan's marriage? A miserable thing, I knew it wouldn't last – but when has Susan ever listened to me? Imagine marrying a truck-driver, what else could she expect? The man was a brute, spent the little he earned on drink. Not that Susan helped much; she has no idea about managing money or keeping a home. In the end he left her because he thought she was having affairs. And I dare say she was.'

'Does she . . . work, I mean, has she a . . . ?'

'Job. Yes. She's a waitress at some greasy spoon where she'll probably meet her next husband. Not that marriage will make one ounce of difference – I shall be supporting her and the two boys for as long as I live. God knows, it's a pity that she ever had children.' I sought Nicola's eyes through smoke. 'Ironical, I should say, that you ought to have had children and didn't, whereas Susan . . .' I gave a shrug of defeat.

'You know, I couldn't . . . have children, I mean, which is just as well, yes, I'm very relieved, especially now.'

'Now?'

But Nicola had turned away from me, her long nose distant and oblique. 'Oh, look, I . . .' She pointed to the arrivals information board: Susan's plane had just landed.

Suddenly I felt pressed for time. Had Nicola taken in the meaning of what I was saying? That Susan needed help, her life had to be changed, and if I could not do it then maybe, somehow, Nicola and Augustus could do something. In the last analysis there was no one else to whom I might turn. But was I turning? It was hardly my way to seek outside assistance. The curious notion came to me, quite illogically, that I had brought Susan here for Nicola's sake, and not the other way around.

When we moved towards the arrivals barrier I took Nicola's hand as if to keep her on my side of it. Though cousins, she and Susan were not meant to be friends; my critical words, it would seem, had been spoken to suggest a great and unbridgeable distance between them. Nicola's hand did not resist mine; it felt cold, nearly dead, yet possessive – as she herself never was. Interesting, I thought, how precisely touch transmits emotion.

Susan saw me before I saw her. My first awareness of her was a frantically waving hand in a sea of trolleys; her need, her bright, tireless love flew straight at me like a besotted parrot. Familiar details followed: the orange hair in Dolly Parton curls, tight jeans, high heels – she wobbled eagerly towards me looking like a part-time call girl in a small town bordello.

No reticence now, no waiting to be spoken to; in the strangeness of her new locality I was all she knew. 'Hi Mom, it sure is good to see you.' And she strained upwards to kiss me. A dwarf, I thought with Nicola tall beside me – Susan's definitely stunted.

I introduced her to her long lost cousin who flinched involuntarily at the thick lipstick and cheap perfume which pressed itself against her cheek in enthusiastic greeting. Rather like a duchess bending down to a peasant, I thought, with the usual bitter amazement and shame that such a squat round woman could be my child. Why had I not had the other one? Why was Nicola not my daughter?

'I'm really glad to meet you, Nicola. Mom's told me so much

about you, guess she thinks you're someone special. Well, you're the only family she's got.' She paused, but a reply did not come quickly enough to prevent her rattling on. Compulsively. 'Golly, you know it gives me goose bumps just thinking about it, me here in London. Never dreamed I'd ever get further than Chicago, now here I am. I sure was busy the last few days, getting ready. Those boys of mine, no clean clothes and then they wanted to buy presents for their dad, well, I can tell you I was darn well rushed off my feet . . .'

I had to interrupt; she would never have stopped of her own accord. 'Susan, must you gabble? As for the clean clothes and presents, I seem to recall that I took care of that.'

She gave me a weak pink-lipped grin, her way of cringing like a dog which has been kicked, and at once I felt angry, unfairly accused – must Susan forever put me in the wrong?

'Let me help you with the . . .' Nicola took hold of Susan's trolley which I noticed was overloaded with luggage; far more than was needed for a short stay.

'Looks like you've brought everything but the kitchen sink, honey. How much was the overweight bill?'

Susan looked at me in a puzzled way as she trotted after Nicola pushing the trolley. Her plump defenceless bottom wobbled as did her ample bust in its tight pink Angora sweater. Yet her hair – so loud and crude an orange, and natural, no chemical excuses – beneath its sleazy curls shone out bright messages of joy. What was it about Susan? That thing I could not touch, her life, the core of it in which was lodged a fragment of pure happiness such as only the simple, the religious or remarkable possess. Another way in which she was not my daughter.

'Overweight, Mom?' But she was beginning to redden, and glanced down inadvertently at her thighs as if it were her poundage under discussion. Alerted by the tone of my voice Nicola had looked round: was I sharper than I realized?

'Yes, overweight. Why so many suitcases?'

Susan looked enormously relieved. 'It's all right, Mom. Most of them aren't mine.'

I frowned. 'Whose then?' I was already suspicious, spotting in advance some sort of muddle or complication such as Susan always brought to the simplest of arrangements.

'Scottie's. He's over at Avis renting us a car.'

I already knew before she spelt it out that Susan had taken it upon herself to come accompanied, no doubt by some lout she had recently picked up; and without the slightest notion of common courtesy towards myself or Nicola. Did she not know, at the age of thirty, that extra guests ought to be invited or at least announced in advance?

'Oh for heaven's sake, Susan. What on earth have you done this time? You've brought someone with you, haven't you?'

'I didn't think you'd mind, Mom.' Her face was already brighter than her hair; a startled, shocked sort of shade as though my gathering anger were a total surprise. 'Scott's a sweet guy. You'll like him.' Susan has no memory (which I suppose explains why she loves me); my previous reaction to her taste in men was simply not there to inform the present situation.

Nicola had stopped pushing and was watching us from a few feet off with a curious expression. Her face long and thoughtful, her nose judgemental, in her black cloak she looked like a figure of justice. Yet justice held no interest for her: having perceived and somehow classified the friction between Susan and me her face took on a look of odd satisfaction which was slightly cunning, and I thought to myself, yes, she is glad. For the same reason that I was glad of friction between her and Augustus.

She was also embarrassed, as the English are by 'scenes' in public. She twiddled with the one long earring she was wearing until a bit of it came off in her fingers. She glanced down with astonishment at the evidence of damage in her hand.

Meanwhile I was deciding what to do. Which was enormously

difficult. I could not think, I was immobilized with anger. How could Susan do this to me, why must she punish me again and again? She meant to spoil my plans, to ruin everything. That man, whoever he was, must be got rid of at once.

And yet, when I saw him, I began to change my mind.

Susan was close to tears, her features starting to crumple, her make-up smudged in advance. Like someone in the last stages of drowning she flapped a hand hopelessly towards a tall man approaching. Her introductions were pathetic. 'Mom, Nicola, meet Scottie. Sure is cute, isn't he?'

Cute he was not. 'Jesus, knock it off, will you!' was how he took her foolish flattery and obvious distress.

Scott was a cowboy, a farm labourer, a trucker – who knows? A bar-room brawler basically, content to drift and damage; I suspected a criminal record because I knew this type from years of meeting Susan's men. Why did she do it? Why choose abuse when she might have been like Nicola and married stability? I could have found her doctors, lawyers, decent professionals with money and manners – instead she preferred the dregs of society. 'Mom, you married Dad, and he sure wasn't educated': this was Susan's excuse but her real reason was me; bad men pushed me away, demonstrated loudly her refusal of my values, which were all I could give her in place of love. And which she could not take for that reason.

Therefore Scott. He stood before us tall and ominous like a huge pine about to come crashing down. Grey eyes cruel and flecked with red, his gaze was inimical while his huge red hands mimed aggression, one fist rhythmically pounding into the palm of the other, over and over again. He was wearing the inevitable blue jeans and checked shirt with a shoelace necktie, and where his shirt opened at the throat the tattoo of something unpleasant emerged from the lower regions of his body. The smell of him I knew all too well – perspiration, hair oil, cheap aftershave. And another thing: old misery, stale unhappiness – the kind that is never washed clean.

This took my attention, not out of pity but because it might be useful. The man would make trouble, and perhaps I should let him. Perhaps Nicola and Augustus – especially Augustus, so responsive to all ills – should see Susan at her worst through this least healthy of relationships. How else would they realize just how badly she needed help? I saw possibilities in Scott and let him be, let him stay, but not without preliminary goading.

I took the trolley from Nicola and pushed it at him. 'You take the luggage in the car. We'll go by taxi and see you back at the house. Nicola will give you the address.'

'Mom . . .' Susan started to protest but I gripped her arm very tightly; she knew my grip, she was silenced.

Nicola began a complicated attempt at direction. 'You go right at the . . . and when you see a petrol station go left until . . . though it's not quite as far as one thinks, so it's best to move into the . . .'

I moved towards the door with Susan in tow, confident that Scott would be too mystified to vent his spleen on Nicola.

Outside, once again at the taxi rank, I said to Nicola, 'You have grasped the situation, I trust? Susan here has brought you an additional houseguest. He may not be a charmer but at least he has rarity value. "Nostalgie de la boue" might be another way of putting it. But still.'

Nicola looked totally drained and grey. The black of her cloak sought out shadows about the face. She glanced at me as if to say: what has all this to do with you and me? It is us this is about, not these strangers. I gazed back at her the answer that they had their place in the scheme of things. She lit another cigarette and waited.

NINE

❧❧❧❧❧❧❧❧❧❧❧❧❧❧❧❧❧

All the way back in the taxi Susan peered through the window and from time to time commented enthusiastically, if ungrammatically, on what she saw; that no one responded did not seem to spoil her pleasure. With her small-minded talent for living in the immediate present, she had forgotten already our altercation at the airport, and the vengeful anger Scott would certainly be storing up for later, if and when he managed to find Augustus's house.

Nicola, for her part, seemed to have forgotten Susan. Absolutely still and quiet on the other side of me, I felt her thinking. But about what? Though I could not read her thoughts it seemed to me that I was included in them; Susan's alien and intrusive presence had somehow heightened the sense of intimacy, even complicity, between us.

Halfway home Nicola glanced around at Susan, judged her preoccupied, and began to tell me what it was that had been on her mind. She spoke in a low confidential whisper, more fragmented and uneven than her ordinary speaking voice, so that I had to lean in closely to catch each word.

'I don't think I ever told you about what happened to Matty . . . ten years ago, yes, it must have been, because I was in hospital then . . . and the thing was, that I didn't realize for quite a while that anything was wrong.'

'What was wrong?'

'I suppose one might call it a . . . breakdown of sorts.'

'What sort?'

'A mental readjustment, really, which . . . it was actually a kindness at the time more than an illness, and the curing of it definitely dreadful for her.' She felt around for her braid and stroked it the way some people will seek comfort from cats.

It started with letters from Africa which reached Nicola during her long convalescence. They were different from anything Mother had written before because they were about love.

'She wrote, in her beautiful small precise hand, that she was in love for the first time in her life . . . just when she was sure it could never ever happen to her because of . . . though it wasn't just her father's fault, of course, it was also her own independence of spirit resulting from his abdication, you see, she had little respect for most men she met.'

'Surely seventy must have seemed a bit old to fall in love. It's not quite the thing one does at that age.' (At the age of fifty-nine I considered seventy a time of life beyond all emotion – now I doubt that such a state exists, ever.)

Nicola looked at me with Mother's sideways sweep along the cheekbones. 'I must admit I was surprised but . . . I wanted to believe her because it held out hope for me though . . . I wanted to believe it for her sake too, and I was sure that she was unusual enough and strong enough to do such a thing, fall in love at seventy.'

Apparently Mother wrote a series of letters in rapid succession; the number and frequency of them ought to have alerted Nicola at once to something being wrong – but she was ill at the time, and it was not long since Angela had died – she needed fantasy. Mother described with girlish enthusiasm and in relentless detail the course of her affair; soppy, sentimental stuff was how it sounded yet Nicola had absorbed it like a sponge. Waited with bated breath for each new instalment.

At around this same time Nicola met Augustus who was assigned to her case, and she found that she could not help applying Mother's situation to her own.

'Because, I suppose, this man she was in love with . . . the only fact she ever gave me as a clue to his identity was that he was a doctor, so I . . . wishful thinking, of course, that my doctor might be hers, might come to mean the same thing to me as hers did . . . mind you, women often become infatuated with their physicians.'

'God knows why. It's as bad as marrying one's dentist. But how did you realize that the letters were not what they seemed?'

Her long nose quivered with the quickness of defence. 'They *were* what they seemed, I mean . . . quite sincere, she meant what she wrote, it was just that her sense of reality had gone, temporarily, that is . . .'

'What do you mean?'

'She was living in the past.' Nicola risked a quick look at Susan, found her suitably oblivious; then continued in a conspiratorial way as if things would be said no one else ought to hear. Matters private to her and me. 'I can understand that you might not like this idea of . . . Matty falling in love, but let me assure you it in no way undid the past because it was the past, and that is why I thought you ought to know, you see, it shows how much he meant to her . . . she simply could not let go so she imagined it happening again and . . . embroidered a little, added in what she wished had happened.'

'And what might that have been?' My scepticism was becoming irritation, not at Nicola but at the situation – to make so much of an old woman's fantasies was hardly worthwhile.

'On the envelopes, return address, you know, she started to call herself Mrs Matty English . . . of course I was puzzled because . . . but then a letter came from Kumar which said that . . .'

'She was crazy.'

'Oh, I would hardly put it that way.' Her eyes were mildly reproachful. 'Senile dementia was the diagnosis . . . brought on by anaemia . . . she was treated in the end, and when her mind was better she had a mild stroke, it was the shock, you see, of returning to reality, so sad.'

'Sadder still if such mental lapses are hereditary. I shall have to watch myself.'

'I suppose that's true, Hermione, perhaps . . .' She looked at me absent-mindedly as if suddenly remembering forwards instead of backwards, and seeing no difference in it. Her eyes registered relief without knowing its details.

Nicola's vague and patchy way of speaking, though pregnant with meaning on familiar subject matter, on the unfamiliar could be totally mystifying. And now, whispering so that Susan mightn't hear (the inconvenience of a third party seemed merely to spur her on) she was particularly incoherent, not just acoustically but also because, for some reason, she was uncertain – about whether she ought to say what she was saying, and perhaps about her motivations.

Her story of Mother's senile dementia confused and bothered me; preyed on my mind without permission. Later that day when I tried to unravel what she said by writing it into my diary, it wrote up poorly because there was something I did not wish to know. If Nicola was mildly incomprehensible, then I, her listener, was uncomprehending, but for a particular reason.

Nicola had said, and I could not forget, 'I thought you ought to know, you see, it shows how much he meant to her'. So who was 'he'? Not the fantasy figure, the doctor called English, but the original version with whom Mother was 'living in the past' – for this was what I decided Nicola must have meant: some lover in the past became the model for an imaginary lover whom she named Dr English – she had simply given him a familiar name, the first one to hand. But who was he really?

I recalled my adolescent fears and suspicions that a lover existed; Nicola seemed to be telling me I was right after all. If so, I did not want to know it, and my rival, the usurper, would not have a name. His identity was not my business, his very existence anathema. Surely ignorance, that much protection, was my right. Yet Nicola was keen to resurrect the past and seemed to assume that this man was so familiar to me that he did not need naming.

Avoiding the question I would not ask, I did make a few other queries before we reached home.

'What started it, do you know? Mother's breakdown or senile dementia, whatever it was.'

'His death . . . he was her neighbour at the beach . . . I think perhaps you never knew that, you see, Mummy didn't because . . . it was our secret, Matty asked me not to tell.'

'A neighbour? Well, I suppose at her age and in her state of health the death of one of her fish might have done the trick.'

'Perhaps but . . .' She looked suddenly surprised, confused by my responses.

'Darling, why did you tell me this story? I know it makes a good anecdote, but why bring it up?'

Nicola looked bewildered. 'I suppose because yesterday I said nothing about him . . . I mean, your . . .'

'Well, Mother's neighbours have never meant a thing to me.'

'Neighbours . . . but we are talking about your . . .' She looked at me carefully, distanced and considering. Then aghast. 'It would be so sad if you never knew . . . I just assumed . . . but then, I knew nothing about it until after Matty's illness, it was only then that she explained, and I suppose after so many years of secrecy it's hardly . . .'

'I don't follow you.'

I did not want to follow. I was absolutely shut to meaning and Nicola, perceiving this, fell silent.

I concluded crisply, 'Mother in love. Whether or not it was pure senile fantasy or something to do with her past relived, I'm afraid it's all a nonsense, darling, as far as I'm concerned. Mother never loved anyone in her life. Except herself.'

Yet I felt the glow of jealousy fiercely, I remembered well the heat of resentment and dread. If there was one thing I would not discuss it was this, Mother loving someone else, love which ought to be mine going elsewhere. But now Nicola knew, saw the pain it caused me; we would not come this way again.

Susan interrupted us and for once I was grateful to her. 'This must be London already. I sure am excited. You know, Mom, we got to buy something nice for the boys. It's kind of sad that they won't be seeing all this.' (So far we had seen nothing but motorway and distant suburbs.)

'Next time, honey.'

She adjusted her bra strap thoughtfully. 'I can't imagine what it's like to live here. Seems so unreal, like something out of Disneyland. But you lived here, Mom, didn't you, for a while?'

'England was never home. Which is not to say that I don't consider myself English. Or perhaps I should say British.'

Susan nodded sagely as if what I had said was profoundly significant. Nicola next to me sighed.

TEN

❧❧❧❧❧❧❧❧❧❧❧❧❧❧❧❧❧

It seemed to me highly ironical that Mother should have given her valetudinarian lover, imaginary or perhaps once real, the name of her old family friend and physician. I wrote in my diary that evening: of all the men she knew there was none less likely to have shared her bed than Dr English. I could vouch for that – I knew – I had watched them together for as long as I could remember. Had there been the slightest hint of amorous connection I would have been upon it instantly.

I wrote: theirs was a tranquil and steady friendship, the only such one, come to think of it, in Mother's life. After all, people came and went in Kenya – moved on to Tanganyika or South Africa, returned to England for reasons of health or finance. There was little continuity in relationships because few acquaintances continued to be accessible. Dr English was the only exception to this rule, and he was in and out of Mother's life from Angela's birth until she left Njoro, turning up every few months to visit her or treat someone for fever. They were so familiar with each other that, together, they relaxed into a form of calm indifference. Oh yes, they knew each other far too well to be lovers.

During my last few years at Njoro when my suspicions of Mother were at their height, I welcomed Dr English's presence – to the extent that I ever welcomed anyone's – as a diversion, a way of drawing Mother away from the men who threatened to take her from me. I knew that whenever he was around he would hold her full attention so that she had no time for others.

Those others: I watched them, I tracked them round the farm when I was supposedly hunting, and thought about how I might shoot them instead – 'it was an accident', would be my excuse, or 'I mistook him for a reedbuck'. In the cover of the grey-bearded cedar forest I was a solitary, vengeful figure flitting from tree to tree. And at night, after dinner, I would sit in the darkest corner of the living room watching and listening for evidence. Had I found it what would I have done? My visions of retribution tended to be along the lines of natural disaster – Menengai Crater erupting, terrible floods rising up from the valley, cholera taking us by surprise.

But when Dr English was with us the volcano turned dormant, the floods subsided and disease was banished; he was a doctor of superior powers – he warmed Mother, he lulled me. He stayed with us every few months on his medical rounds because our farm was a halfway point between Naivasha, his base, and Kisumu at the edge of his territory. Though he had been our general practitioner in the old days at Naivasha, and indeed ever since on a friendly basis, his job during those latter years seemed to be administrative rather than clinical and I supposed he was some sort of health inspector.

Nonetheless he advised Mother on many other matters: agricultural problems, how to tackle a bank manager in Nairobi, what to do about the wolfhound's sore paw. He brought her fruit from the coast, butterflies, Chanel Number Five and silk stockings. For Angela and me there was always something like a book or Indian sweets or ribbons, and I liked to think that my presents were always just slightly nicer than Angela's – as if he preferred me – but this notion was influenced by Angela's reserve with him; she was never quite glad when he came. Which made me even more pleased to see him. I noticed that Jock Weaver was also less than enthusiastic about Dr English's frequent presence at our farm; but Jock was so often away his opinion hardly mattered.

This fact was sometimes commented upon by Dr English

when he and Mother were discussing the running of the farm.

'I shall have to consider very hard whether or not to clear another acre of forest for wheat. The prices are such that it hardly seems worthwhile, and then there is the problem of labour. I have barely enough men as it is, and no one else to supervise. Now if we could afford a manager, my problems would be over.'

'If Jock spent a bit more time at home you wouldn't need a manager, Matilda. Have you discussed the situation with him? Does he understand?' Dr English smoked a pipe; each sentence was punctuated by a thoughtful puff.

'Oh, you know what Jock's like. He's a child, really, a small boy who's never grown up. He doesn't want to understand. Only interested in his safaris, but still, there you are. Can't expect a leopard to change his spots, can you now?' Mother flicked away flies as if her problems were equally inconsequential.

'Be that as it may, you have taken on too much, my dear. Jock ought to realize.'

'Well, Rupert, you know me, I like a bit of adversity and challenge. Let me put it this way – I would not like to feel I could not manage on my own. Leave Jock be, let him play, he's irrelevant.'

They had a way together, Mother and Dr English, that happened with no one else. There was an ease of manner between them as if they were family, say, brother and sister or close cousins. Mother's voice warmed an octave and her icy poise relaxed a little into casual attitudes. She would lean forward on her elbows when she talked to him, a confidential position, no sideways aloofness; and no cigarettes – she forgot to smoke or felt no need for a smoke screen.

I remember them like this quite clearly because it had an effect on me. My sharp attention began to blur into something approaching a sense of well-being – they were like family together so I felt a family feeling. Which never lasted long, of course; it was simply a flash of understanding that other children enjoyed a sense of harmony and peace at home. Unfortunately I was not other children.

Had I ever entertained the slightest doubt about Mother and Dr English, I had only to look at him to be reassured. He was not Mother's type, he was physically incompatible. Next to her tall and slim willowy form he was stocky and short, plebeian, ponderous, a work horse with a thoroughbred, out-classed. Nonetheless there was virtue in this: his sturdy body and steady looks radiated calm reliability – here was a man who was always predictable, steadfast, totally trustworthy (and there were not very many who might answer to that description). A rock of a man without rough edges, he had a face like a smoothed down boulder, rounded, features minimal; though his eyes were quietly remarkable, rather large and a deep warm brown. Dog's eyes, I used to call them. He was pleasant in appearance, very easy to look at but hardly handsome. Whereas Mother's husbands were all tall and suave with their little moustaches and fashionable clothes.

For as long as I knew him Dr English never changed. He grew neither fatter nor slimmer, wore the same clothes and smoked the same pipe. Here was a man to be taken for granted, forgotten from time to time and then happily rediscovered. He was a constant.

If Dr English advised Mother on her handling of the farm, he also gave out advice about the management of children. Me, in particular. I would eavesdrop.

'She hates me,' Mother would say, running red fingernails through her black hair. 'Hermione hates me and what can I do against that? She is punishing me but I don't know why. If I knew, if I could only understand . . . oh, it's all so unfair, and her of all children. She has become so difficult there is nothing I can do. There are no opportunities even to try to . . . put things right.' Her voice was slightly less than clear, there were minute hesitations in delivery which only occurred when she talked about me.

He drew on his pipe, concerned and considering. 'Actually she loves you. Rather too much. In her world there are only two people: herself and you.'

'That is not entirely surprising. She has never been given the third, not properly.'

He considered without passion her words and replied: 'There are many children in the world without fathers.'

'Yes, but hers is special. She knows this, she knows she is deprived.'

'It's you she feels deprived of. She wants too much. Something in her nature, Matilda.'

'Perhaps if I hadn't felt I had to hide. Do you think that's it? The habit of hiding so that no one would suspect? She feels that I am withholding myself from her – but I did it for her sake, had to do it, and now it's a habit, I suppose.'

'She's a lot like your father.'

'Ah yes, and you know how very close we were, he and I, before it all started. I wish that Hermione and I . . .'

He nodded. He knew everything about her. They had had this conversation over and over again, in different forms though the content was unchanging. Because there were no solutions, no insights: neither knew what to do about me. Dr English had a standard conclusion:

'All we can do is accept her as she is. And let her go easily when she wants to leave. The risk of unfinished relationships is that it's hard to let go of them, one cannot admit defeat, one is driven to keep on trying.'

'I should have thought, Rupert, that letting go is something I'm good at. Have you ever known me to hold on?'

'My dear, you have always done what had to be done.' And his hand would come out calmly to cover hers.

*

Such talk left me unbearably frustrated, but in a way I could not understand. It seemed to me that the conclusion was never the right one – something else was waiting to be said, hovering in the air. I felt a different ending yet could not describe it. Though I would listen with greed and a certain sense of malice at intruding, my feeling of power would quickly drain away into helplessness: the power was theirs, the power of resolution – so why would they not use it? They stopped short, always, from wherever their conversation was going; while I wanted them to go on yet could do nothing from my hiding place.

Though I refused to listen to Mother when she spoke to me directly, I could not get enough of what she said about me to Dr English. And I was not jealous of her confidential trust in him because he was the only man who posed no threat whatsoever; I could allow him, he would never take Mother away from me.

I can remember only one occasion on which I was ever alone with Dr English. A singularity which seems to indicate avoidance though it never seemed such at the time.

One of Mother's admirers, disillusioned as to his chances, had cornered me on the verandah to complain. He had noticed – could not fail to – my sullen manner and peevish comments in Mother's presence. Assuming sympathy he said to me,

'You know, Hermione, I feel sorry for you. I have to admit it used to be your mother I felt sorry for, but now I can see why you're bitter. She cares for no one but herself.' I said nothing so he continued, his voice uneasy but determined, persistent. 'She thinks herself so superior, those aristocratic airs she puts on, she thinks she's too good to be bothered with people like me . . .'

I interrupted viciously. 'That's because she is too good for people like you. God knows why she puts up with you at all. Typical, isn't it? You eat her food, enjoy her hospitality and then criticize behind her back. How dare you!'

He was shocked, tried to look amused. 'I say, a chip off the old block.' And he shuddered slightly as he met my eye with misplaced lust, a mistake he could not rectify until after it was over. I was tall, nearly his height, but a thin child in build and asexual. He said, 'You don't like men, do you?'

'I certainly don't like you.'

I was wound up, feeling the power of my own indomitable resistance: no one would overcome me, no man could get the better of me. Yet he had done a certain damage, I felt cornered, rather desperate. Tears that must not show were gathering.

As if he knew I needed rescuing – though in actual fact he must simply have been passing by – Dr English appeared with his comfortable pipe, appraised the situation quickly and astutely. 'Ah, there you are, Hermie, I've been looking everywhere for you.' (He never looked for me, nobody did.) 'Will you excuse us, George? I have something special to show Hermione.' My opponent nodded ill-humouredly and Dr English led me away.

We walked together across the lawn towards the herbaceous border because he said there was a small animal rustling around there and quite possibly wounded. 'I said to myself, here's a job for Hermie. No one else has such a way with animals. You know, my dear, you ought to be a vet. Or a doctor – people are animals too, after all, look at it that way.'

'Healing doesn't interest me much.'

'I dare say, at your age.' He puffed at his pipe. Then added enigmatically, 'Well, time heals all.' I could feel that he was searching about for words and not finding them, as people without children often do when confronted by conversation with a minor.

Careful watching and listening about the canna lilies revealed nothing. He smiled at me his steady, imperturbable smile. 'It must have gone,' he said.

And then he was gone too. As doctors will once crises are over; silently, swiftly, seeking out new need. But I felt that he had let me down: I expected more, much more. Somehow our encounter seemed unfinished, incomplete, though I had no idea what I might have expected of him. At least a new animal – but not this standing alone in the darkening garden when twilight is so swift in the tropics.

On another occasion, he said to me, 'You have beautiful eyes, Hermie. Beautiful brown eyes.'

He was looking from Mother to Angela to me. Blue eyes, green eyes, brown eyes. I waited – surely this was only the start, an introduction. But he took out his pipe and drew on it calmly; not his place, apparently, to comment further. Yet I liked to think afterwards that there was an element of restraint in all this; he wanted to say I was beautiful even though I could find no beauty in myself.

ELEVEN

✤✤✤✤✤✤✤✤✤✤✤✤✤✤✤✤✤✤

Augustus was at home when we returned from the airport though he did not make his presence known at once. He was working in his study. As we took off our coats in the narrow hallway, he appeared suddenly, waving a rolled up periodical.

'Look, darling, I found it. The article on *myocardial ischaemia*.'

'Oh, super, I . . .' Fluted murmurs of gladness from Nicola.

I took it upon myself to handle introductions. 'This is my daughter, Susan.'

She hung back a bit in the gloomy hallway as if unsure that I wanted her seen; like some tawdry statuette, a sleazy souvenir unwisely purchased as a last minute gift. Yet when Augustus shook her hand she emerged into the light and assumed an unwonted integrity; for a start he made sense of her size – the two of them in build are not dissimilar – and I thought to myself, why does she always choose huge men like Scott? So much bigger than she is, he makes her look ridiculous.

Augustus was heartily welcoming. 'Super, absolutely marvellous of you to come all this way. How are you? One can get dreadfully tired on long-haul flights. It's the dehydration, you know, more than lack of sleep.'

He chatted on reassuringly in his plummy voice, bedside manner automatic.

And Susan was put at her ease very readily. 'I sure am glad to meet you. Guess I've never met a doctor out of hospital before. It's kind of exciting to have one in the family.' She paused for a moment, cocked her head to one side and added,

'Maybe I should call you Gus. Augustus is a real mouthful of a name.'

He laughed royally. 'Yes, marvellous, call me Gus. Friends always do. Super.'

Susan liked him, I could see that, though not what she liked in him. And in response to that decision she began to do what she does with most men (for she likes most men she meets) – she offered herself, inappropriately, abruptly, and for no other reason except that he was an acceptable man and she knew no other way. I suppose many women flirt on acquaintance in one way or another but Susan with her simple mind was hardly subtle: eyelashes fluttered, hips gyrated – nothing original in her signals of attraction.

Augustus seemed unaware of designs on his person. He was looking at something else about her and the clinical eye ran deeper. I detected a heightening of colour; suppressed excitation. Aroused he was, though not in the way Susan wished.

I knew what he had seen, or rather, that he had seen right through her. Because there was nothing in the centre of Susan, no backbone, nothing firm. She was selfless in the oldest sense of having no self. She desired, for the most part, nothing more than to be what others desired; if she wanted anything at all it was only to be wanted. A definition of goodness perhaps but hardly sound character. Recently, I must say, Susan has firmed up a bit but then her amorphousness appalled and punished me; that my daughter could be so resolutely weak was ample retribution for all my maternal sins.

Yet Augustus gleamed. He had found something valuable. He reminded me of an octopus just come upon an empty jar. What wonderful home was this for his wandering spirit, a woman who would mould herself to his psychic requirements. Would she perform for him the role of perfect patient – someone permanently ill and needing his ministrations, yet perpetually responsive to treatment? A slave to his obsessive urge to heal?

He blushed.

Aha, I thought, so Nicola is not the perfect patient any more, he is frustrated, he's looking elsewhere.

Susan spotted need at once. She moved in until her bust almost touched his chest. 'I sure hope you're not going to be working over Christmas, Gus. Just tell them at the hospital that we can't spare you. That's what Dad used to do.'

I was surprised that she would mention her father to a stranger. Indeed, 'father' has never been a word with much currency in our family – I never say it; neither, I noticed, did Nicola.

Augustus, who was not a father, suddenly looked to me so strange, so alien, that I could hardly believe we belonged to the same species. No wonder Nicola never had children, I thought, and for a moment (though these are matters I prefer not to think about) I doubted that they could ever have had what is termed a full sexual relationship.

Nicola watched the encounter between Augustus and Susan with some interest. Her unfocused half-smile never wavered, her sleepy eyelids remained negligent and vague – there was not the slightest trace of anxiety in her mild expression, and I thought: she really does not mind at all, in fact, one might almost think her pleased. She stood near them absent-mindedly toying with her bracelets, then wandered off towards the kitchen.

I wondered, might she be glad to relinquish her role to another? I remembered the pantomime between herself and Augustus the night before and how her knuckles had shown white at the strain of his wishes – she was weary of their contract, had outgrown it in some way. Another man, another interest? Unlikely, but something was changed and Nicola had hidden it.

Did she always dissimulate? It occurred to me then that Nicola's imprecise attitudes might well be a convenient means of removal. A slender chance at privacy, those unfinished sentences and vague, distant looks. Less a ploy than a means of survival meticulously developed over the years against the demands and intrusions of others – and both Angela and Augustus were undoubtedly demanding in their very different ways. In return Nicola had made herself aloof. And self-sufficient: for if she secretly deplored the demands of others, she would not wish to duplicate dependency by demands of her own.

Self-sufficient individuals do not make good patients; they decline to ask for help, might refuse it if offered, and a cure at any cost may well not seem worthwhile. Nicola, I was sure, had ceased to be her husband's patient the day she left hospital – but did he know this? Or had she sustained the necessary illusion of needing his hungry skills because this was the only need he recognized? There were two categories of people in Augustus's world: himself and the ill crying out for help. So where did this leave Nicola?

It left her leaving, gliding away gladly towards the kitchen. She was wearing a long, lacey skirt (perhaps a recycled tablecloth) and beneath it her tread was light, considerably lightened, as if all the fatigue of the morning had fallen away from her.

Scott managed far better than I would have thought possible and arrived shortly after we did. But his temper had not been improved by the exigencies of map reading, driving on the left side of the road, and dealing with big city traffic.

'Hi, sweetie,' Susan greeted him brightly.

He bellowed back at her, not caring who else heard, 'Just what the sam-hell did you think you were doing, going off and leaving me? Next time you pull a stunt like that . . .' He left what he would do to the imagination.

'I'm really sorry, Scottie, it's just that Mom . . .'

He cut her short. 'Yes, your mother all right, she's the one.' But he did not elaborate, I was standing too near.

Susan shifted on her high heels nervously, adjusted a bra strap, then gave him a pink submissive smile. A toy, I thought, nothing but a toy in the hands of worthless men.

And what would Augustus make of this crudely hewn primitive Susan had brought with her? His reaction to the relationship was what interested me: I awaited lunch with eager anticipation.

I had to wait rather longer than expected as Nicola had problems in the kitchen. Perhaps it was our swollen numbers – I had never seen her so disorganized. Chaos compounded, all the necessary elements of a meal were there scattered about amid the jars and papers and jewellery, it was just that she could not seem to assemble them. Without my help.

She made various excuses. 'It's meat, you know. I simply can't bear meat any more, not even to prepare it, not that anything else . . . of course I knew the appetite would go, hardly surprising, and I really don't mind, it's the . . .'

'Is the ham in the fridge?' I could see that Nicola was going to need considerable assistance throughout Christmas, and added rather irritably, 'I did say you ought to lie down when we got back.'

She glanced back offhandedly. 'Oh, it makes no difference, you know . . .'

After what seemed to be far more effort than lunch deserved, the table was set and duly laden with food. Augustus ambled noisily out of his study, Susan appeared from the bathroom where she had been applying new layers of make-up, and Scott extricated himself from a narrow armchair in front of the television to complain, 'What's happened to the football?' When nobody answered he migrated to a chair at the table which cracked its joints at the brutal weight of him.

Susan sat down next to him. 'How's your appetite, sweetie?'

He gave her a lewd look. 'Good enough to eat you whole.' But then he remembered his priorities. 'Hey, what's happened to the football? I got to watch the match. They told me our football gets on British TV, so where is it? I darn well ain't gonna miss it.' He was seriously concerned, becoming aggrieved (and lapsed into dialect accordingly).

Augustus pretended to be helpful. 'The only American football I know of comes on television around eleven at night. You might try later.'

'Later? You mean it's not live?' He turned to Susan accusingly. 'Jesus, why didn't you tell me?' His face was growing red, the tattoo at his collarbone darkening frightfully as colour ran down to his chest.

'Oh for heaven's sake,' I interposed, 'how on earth could she know? Anyhow, I can't think why you expected to watch it now – you've obviously forgotten the time change. Or can't subtract.' I was backing him into a corner but undecided as yet how far to go.

'I sure as hell wouldn't have come if I'd known.' His voice was ominous, his hands nervy and frustrated; he cracked his knuckles loudly like a gun going off.

'Then it's a pity somebody didn't tell you.'

It took a while for my meaning to come to him. When it did, he glanced at me furiously, then turned his feelings on Susan. She was the one he blamed, she had brought him to a foreign place where he felt ill at ease and insulted, foolish and ignorant. This reaction went way back, I could tell; he had seen himself inferior, shown up to be deficient or even laughable for most of his life. He struck out blindly against the taunting unfairness of everything, and at Susan in particular as if she had authorized it all. 'You sure are one helluva stupid . . .' he began.

'I think you'd like some wine.' Augustus stopped him immediately with quiet but absolute authority. The words were irrelevant – it was the tone of voice which counted and which said, quite clearly: that is enough, I will have no more of it. Scott quailed, caved in, with the baffled shame and useless rage such class of person always feels towards the better educated in control of their lives. 'I guess so,' he replied in a last-ditch attempt to salvage his dignity.

'I shouldn't think Scott drinks wine,' I put in casually. 'Beer and whiskey are what men from his part of the world commonly consume.'

Augustus frowned at me, moved around the table, and stood with his body between Susan and Scott while he poured out the wine. He anticipated further misplaced vengeance and his stout form was protective, guarding from harm his new relative by marriage. I sensed in this the slightest element of rivalry, less of one man to another than of one doctor to another (though Scott was a spoiler not a healer). I imagined Augustus competing for a patient with another consultant, implying by every look and touch that his competitor would kill this person whom only he might cure; the careful way he dispensed wine to Susan said just this of Scott's attachment.

From which I deduced that the thing was done: Augustus had taken on Susan, or would soon do so. She was beginning to be his responsibility. Competition, I thought with some satisfaction, is not a bad thing; Scott was serving a purpose.

At the end of lunch Augustus announced to Nicola that he would have to pop out to buy drinks. She nodded inattentively. 'Super, darling, I . . .'

'Take Susan,' I said at once. 'I am sure she needs to buy a few things. What have you forgotten, honey? Toothbrush, hairbrush? Now's your chance.'

Susan looked surprised, she was flushed from wine and lack of sleep. 'I can't think of anything, Mom. I'd kind of like to rest a bit after lunch.'

I fixed her with a steady gaze and read into it my sheer determination. She must go with Augustus, she must talk with him. Her obtuse reticence was infuriating, made me desperate. Why was she doing this to me when so much was at stake? Did she not realize? Must she thwart me on this issue of her own welfare? I would not let her undo what I knew to be essential; she would go with him, she must; it had to be this way. I was prepared to use any means. If you don't go, my eyes said to her, you are selfish and do not love me – must I always be tied to unhappy motherhood?

Susan looked bewildered, apprehensive, then apologetic and pleading; she looked back at me the way she used to when she came home each week with gifts. She glanced around the table and said, for everyone to hear, 'You know, you're right, Mom. Guess I forgot my toothbrush. I'd better go out and buy one.'

Nicola rose from the table and stood like a lazy question mark, her back arched, her head back, her wandering gaze somewhere on the shadowed ceiling. 'Darling, perhaps you should show Susan the walk along the . . . there are a few sights around here, and it's a shame to rush back.' Her breathy voice was firmly encouraging as it echoed back from the pictures of the river on the wall.

No suggestion was made by anyone that Scott might go too.

Nicola and I cleared the table, washed the dishes – no dish-washer in this frugal, antiquated household. Silence fell between us easily because there was so much to be said, and which had been said already.

Still enjoying a remission of fatigue, Nicola flowed about between the dining room and kitchen with a lightness which bore her continuously towards me, coming and going but coming closer every time. She seemed to find it less irksome to clear food away than provide it; she hummed a little – I was pleasantly surprised, I had never heard music come out of her before.

I thought to myself, she is feeling so much better, and realized with it that I had avoided feeling worried when I was. But now she was well again, active, singing. Ready for Christmas. And yet, when I considered how slender she was beneath her gypsy draperies, how thin her wrists – this suddenly struck me – I thought: she needs me, she is so delicate, she needs me to care for her. Then, as if those words had unbidden powers of invention, I knew I was beginning to love her.

Love? When had I ever loved before? Unpractised, it hardly seemed possible to start at my age when dogs had been all of my attachment in the past.

While I was drying the last of the glasses, I watched Nicola's aquiline profile, the nose, the forehead, the distant expression behind the half-smile. It was the face of my lifetime, the face behind mine. She felt my gaze and quickened heartbeat and glanced round defensively as if looks could kill, as if mine had deadly energies. But at once the shock went, she was calm, diffused, completely reconciled to what she was.

She said, 'You know, Matty felt towards her father much the same as you towards her, I mean . . . she never forgave him, it's a pity, you know, to hold onto bad feelings to the . . .'

'Grave.' I was becoming used to finishing her sentences. I would finish anything for her, do anything, go anywhere. Perceiving this as though it had always been true, there was a moment between us of such rapport and complicity that our lives seemed crystal clear in all directions. Then Christmas continued, and I suddenly asked her,

'Why did she hate him? That was never clear to me – I always thought my grandfather sounded rather appealing. So what went wrong? Mother's bound to have told you more than she ever told me.'

'Fathers . . .' Nicola sighed. Then began her next story.

TWELVE

❧❧❧❧❧❧❧❧❧❧❧❧❧❧❧❧❧❧

Mother was born in Mangalore where her father, Harold McGovern, was a Collector in the Indian Civil Service. He came from a long line of colonial administrators, was educated at Marlborough and Oxford with the express purpose of keeping to family traditions, and sent out to India despite the fact that the life ahead of him was one to which he was not in the least bit suited. That is, India suited him in a romantic sort of way, but being a civil servant did not. Harold was a poet, had enjoyed some success as such while at Oxford, and nothing else interested him so much as the beauty of words. He was too private an individual to enjoy civic involvement and too stubborn to serve well in any capacity. His unsuitability showed in his postings – small towns in the south, not the sought-after cities of the Punjab or United Provinces.

If Harold never quite fitted his job, my grandmother for her part was not a natural memsahib. She was not terrible enough (by Somerset Maugham's high standards) – not terrible at all, as Nicola told it: she found running servants difficult, she was shy with other wives, stammered badly, and was ill far too often. Poor woman, she ought never to have left England. And no doubt fewer children would have helped – but they kept on coming, six babies in rapid succession, of which none but Mother survived beyond eight years of life. Each beginning and ending undid a little further my grandmother's precarious health and state of mind.

'Hardly surprising, I dare say, that none of us since has been particularly keen on child-bearing.'

'It's ironic, I think, that the most fertile women often make the worst mothers, you see, they were not at all close, Matty and her mother . . . indeed, one might say that Matty never learned about mothers and daughters at all, not as I did and . . .'

Mother was brought up by servants, and in particular by indulgent ayahs for whom the *baba-log* were, if not deities, at least as requiring of deference as their parents. Colonial children never lacked a sense of their own importance, and the confidence which grew from this was fierce, indomitable, unable to countenance defeat. An advantage in later life? Perhaps, particularly if tempered by the right sort of imported nanny. Mother's was German, draconian; a dedicated disciplinarian from whom she learned the advantages of self-control and perseverance.

'The nanny had her reading books by the time she was five and . . .'

'Perhaps that was also her father's doing.'

'Oh yes, he was always involved in her education, he took an active part in . . .'

My grandfather's role in Mother's early life was not only active but central. Dominating. From infancy he decided that she was 'the one' and took her over with an intense and all-absorbing involvement uncommon even between fathers and sons. Just why he singled out Mother from his ever-changing brood is a question of speculation, but she resembled him – lean build, dark hair, blue eyes – and perhaps he craved a mirror image.

'I rather think that he saw her to be the strongest one, the survivor which of course she . . . and later he relied on her, perhaps from the very beginning too.'

'It may be that she was the weakest in one particular way. A fear of singularity – some people have difficulty with "thou" and "I", can't bear the fact of being separate.'

I was not sure exactly what I meant except that Mother must

have encouraged and needed so close a relationship or it would never have happened. Aloof and self-sufficient though she was as an adult – and this may be why she became so much that way – in the beginning there must have been a part of her unusually hungry for love and attachment. Not that I ever saw any residual evidence of such.

For nearly ten years Mother had her father's undivided and devoted attention at particular times of the day, each day.

Morning exercise after *chota hazri* they took together as a walk along the beach. My grandfather liked the sea, its fish and seabirds, and the dhows which followed the shore. Indeed, the sea featured heavily in his poems of that period (which I have been reading recently), and he made up stories for Mother about a flying fish called Frederica (this too has survived among her papers, a thin illustrated notebook, never shown to me when I might have enjoyed it).

My grandfather always took binoculars with him and whenever he spotted anything of interest he would pass them over to Mother to look; that way she learned early the names of indigenous birds and the distinguishing features of boats which came from Arabia or East Africa or Persia.

'Don't tell me the binoculars Mother used were her father's? Typical, isn't it? She never threw anything away.'

'Well, I doubt . . . but he taught her always to wipe off the lenses before putting them away . . . just as she told me when I . . .'

They talked a lot during these early morning walks. My grandfather was a secret pedagogue; it gave him great pleasure to impart information, quote poetry, expound theories about literature or evolution. He seemed to regard Mother as a kind of receptacle for all that he knew and thought; a place to put his mind where it might survive beyond his lifetime. Gratefully she accepted all he told her; she thought him wonderful, incomparable in knowledge and understanding. He tutored her as carefully as if she existed for no other reason than to be his companion always, and she felt that the privilege of bearing his notions, his preferences, bespoke a glittering, euphoric future.

'Emotional incest.'

'No one ever fascinated her quite as much as he did and . . . later it was a question of finding other terms of reference with men . . .'

'And with women? Never had much to do with 'em as far as I can see. Her friends were all men, come to think of it. Pity Angela and I weren't sons.'

'She loved me . . . but, you see, people do evolve, right up to the end, they keep on trying, and . . .'

'Do you mean to say there's hope for me yet?'

'Oh, Hermione, there's always . . . yes, always that . . . why else would you be here if it were not for . . . hope.'

My grandfather would come to Mother's room each night when he got home from the club. Perched on the edge of her bed in evening dress, elegant and slim, he would tell her whom he saw and what he thought of them. Perhaps what he had said. He could be moody in company and taciturn, though his silences were often mistaken for quiet interest; indeed, he acquired a false reputation for being a good listener when in fact his mind was miles away. At other times he suffered from outbursts of excessive charm which dazzled people and then disappointed them when his warmth subsided into cool indifference. He was not consistent.

'Matty was worried by his charm . . . you see, it rather shocked her, such a sudden radiance in public . . . though it was more the people to whom he was charming that troubled her because . . .'

'She was jealous, I dare say.'

'Less that than . . . apprehensive, rather fearful . . . and, you see, she knew what he was, the self-centredness . . .'

*

The ending of their intimacy was not a sudden event but rather a gradual shifting of interest on the part of my grandfather away from the home. Mother knew early on that there was someone else, a new focus; he was a man who had to be closely attached – and if not to her (and certainly not to his wife) then there must be another person who had stolen his heart. Certain of this Mother did suffer jealousy, then she watched and waited in the fear of being alone. To no avail: the morning walks ceased, the bedside chats stopped. He was often away all night, coming back in the early morning or having breakfast at the club.

He began to drink heavily. When he did come home he was often abusive, sometimes violent to servants. And his drinking began to creep into the daytime so that, in the end, there was no time at which he might be relied upon to be sober. Mother tried to cover up for him in little ways: conveying the right orders to servants, showing guests the garden when he was too shaky to walk with them. Of course by this stage his work was suffering, he was losing credibility with colleagues – there was little that Mother could do to forestall his disgrace.

She tried very hard for a long time to win back his attention. She blamed herself for losing it, and for his increasing alcoholism which seemed somehow related to her fall from grace. The love that he felt for someone else was not a kindly love – look what it was doing to him – so how might she save him?

But her striving to please him and help him in small ways gradually gave way to resentment and anger. She began to be very quiet in his presence or occasionally wildly furious.

'He forgot Matty's birthday . . . her tenth, no present . . . and she shouted at him then, for the very first time . . . said she hated him and . . .'

'Once said it was true.'

'She could never forgive him for letting her . . . hate him, that was the worst loss, her love and respect for him . . .'

'She certainly had little of that for her husbands.'

*

117

When Mother was ten the family suddenly left India. There was no planning of it, no gradual transition; almost overnight they left their home in Cochin to travel to Bombay where they awaited the first available passage home.

No explanation was ever given for the sudden flight from that place which had been home. Though their leaving was not uneventful. My grandfather in a drunken finale attempted to set fire to the house at midday. He went with a torch from window to window setting alight the grass blinds which had been lowered against the sun. In his inebriated condition he failed to notice that they were damp – sprayed with water to keep them cool – and so his bonfire was less than spectacular and simply a final humiliation.

Mother knew that the family's departure was a humiliation of them all and a sign of disgrace. It was his doing, his deeds, but she no longer wanted reasons – they would do no good, it was too late for repairs. She hated him and he was indifferent to his favourite child: what could possibly remedy that?

Mother hated England from the moment she arrived in Southampton and felt the fog on her face. It was a place of exile from which she could only wish to leave at the first opportunity. Yet she decided there was something to be learned from the cold, the way faces shut themselves away because of it; chilly people with their mufflers and blue noses looked impregnable. As did hotel managers and her mother's relatives with their distant, icy manners. Freezing people out was a cunning manoeuvre in the day-to-day violence of personal, and impersonal, relationships.

'She began to polarize her personality, I mean, there was the cool exterior and then . . . other feelings which were rather strong but hidden.'

'And just as well, I dare say. Her anger was maniacal.'

'But only to her father, Hermione . . . and to you, because . . .'

'Because I reminded her of him. Can't think why, can you?'

'Oh, I think there is probably quite a lot, I mean . . . looks, and a certain unchecked quality . . .' ('Selfishness, you mean,' I interjected. She did not seem to hear.) 'And similar abilities, like writing, but she would have found all that later, as justification . . . it was really the fact that you rejected her, that was the key . . . like her father, you would not love her any more.'

'I was never aware that I had loved her in the first place. Why should I? She never loved me.'

They lived in London, not well but adequately, managing off the combined private incomes of both parents. My grandfather 'decided' not to work again (from which Mother deduced that no one would employ him) and he devoted his time to poetry and drink, and the occasional translation from Sanskrit or Tamil. When he disappeared for days on end Mother was given to understand that this must be accepted; her mother accepted it, she had chosen the gentle, elevated life of the invalid, a form of monasticism, a relinquishing of responsibility.

Mother became the woman of the house from the very beginning, gradually taking on full responsibility for the running of things. While she did this with stern satisfaction, definite that she must be what neither parent was, a capable and reliable adult, she nonetheless kept to herself clear notions of escape. She would not remain banished in a country she had not chosen, she would not remain unloved in a household which hardly deserved her. She awaited the first opportunity of leaving – which was marriage.

Mother became engaged to Tom Goodenough, who had a farm in Kenya, without her father's consent. She all but eloped with him; told her father a few days in advance that she was leaving (fair warning that he would have to find a new housekeeper).

'She said she was not kind to him . . . that bothered her later

. . . she was abrupt, uncompromising, simply stating facts baldly.'

She expected a scene – her father was adept at making them when drunk enough, or not, as the case may be – but he was very quiet and resigned, apparently expecting what she came to tell him. He said, 'I'm sorry, my dear', though what exactly for was not clear.

'He tried to give her his mother's wedding ring but Matty would not take it, and . . . she regretted that afterwards, years later when . . . it was too late to put things right.'

Too late because, a few years after Mother left England, the house burned down. He was killed in the fire, which he may or may not have started himself; my grandmother was away at the time convalescing in a nursing home – she stayed on there.

'Matty never forgave herself . . .'

'For what?'

'For not being there at the end, at least to . . .'

'Say last rites? I shouldn't think there was much she could have done. I mean to say, she was hardly a fireman.'

'That's not the point, Hermione, as you . . . she was sad that he died without forgiveness, hers for him, his for her . . . it's so important, you see, it would have changed everything, all her memories of him, because we are selective, the emotions choose what . . .'

'He probably loved her after all, despite how things appeared, and she knew that. People are queer – they don't always express themselves well, or they hide things and concealment sets up barriers. Strong feelings between people are always a form of love, despite all evidence to the contrary.'

'Exactly, Hermione, I . . .'

'One thing, Nicola. Why exactly was my grandfather dismissed from the Indian Civil Service? Do you know?'

'Yes, Matty told me, though . . . she only found out after he was dead, I suppose her mother finally told her then.'

'Well, tell me.'

Why was I always the last to know? Something stirred in me, a fear, the shadow of secrets from my time. In the darkening kitchen the narrow space became constricting, airless, claustrophobic. The river beyond was a black sluggish flow, and the current was against me, I could feel its opposition; such useless effort, paddling onwards, when everything else pulls back. You are halfway home, I told myself, half back; you have no choice but to listen.

'It was all about a love affair, you see . . .'

'Not alcohol? You mean there was another misdemeanour? Well, I dare say extramarital affairs were frowned upon. Was he indiscreet?'

'Very, I'm afraid, you see . . . his lover was Indian.'

'How very exotic of him. Didn't they refer to that sort of thing as a "sleeping dictionary"? — must have done his Tamil a world of good. I trust she was pretty and a maharaja's daughter.'

'I'm afraid not, you see, the lover was not a "she" . . .'

'A man? Well, what else, not much left is there, except animals. How very interesting.'

Though I kept my voice casual, I was shocked, profoundly shocked. Not so much by the thing in itself — sex interests me so little that I hardly care about other people's predilections — it was more that she had told me something totally unexpected about a stranger who was nonetheless part of me; his blood ran in my veins, his dreams informed mine with arcane messages. And what of love, what hard refusal on my part was memory of touch and bliss I never knew?

'We are indeed the past . . .' Nicola was thinking about what had been said and why it needed saying.

'But it is we who haunt times gone, by our own choosing — we are the ghosts, not the dead and departed.'

'So much gets transmitted in families, and quite uncon-

sciously, you see, it's the things people never talk about that
. . . exert the greatest power.'

'So here we are, talking. And will it do any good?'

'Perhaps you will see Matty . . . more clearly, and understand
why she behaved towards you as she did, it was all repetition,
you see, old wounds reopening and . . .'

'Mother was displaced in her father's affections by a lover.
Are you implying that was my fate too?'

How strange that I was asking this when I did not want to
know. It seemed as if a terrible recklessness had suddenly
overwhelmed me and I was seized with compulsion to lay
bare information previously shunned – I would have to know
eventually so I may as well know now. The truth was my right
though not mine to refuse.

But it was too late. Susan and Augustus were returning, there
were clumsy noises of congeniality from the hallway. Our time
together over, reluctantly Nicola and I drew apart and walked
off to present commitments.

THIRTEEN

❧❧❧❧❧❧❧❧❧❧❧❧❧❧❧❧❧

Christmas Eve started with snow flurries and ended with light rain. Drizzle, no downpours, just a steady, sad incontinence. Nicola and I spent most of the day in the kitchen, preparing the dinner and making ready for Christmas lunch the next day. From time to time Susan joined us and made ineffective efforts to help in the crowded space. Whatever she did set us back in our progress: her grated carrots were not fine enough, the potatoes she peeled had to be checked for eyes she had forgotten to remove, the pastry she rolled tore and had to be reshaped. She was wearing a brown mohair dress which made her look like a hamster on heels.

She seemed concerned about Nicola, and, when her cousin was out of earshot, said to me, 'I'm kind of worried about her, Mom. Do you think she's all right?'

'Of course she's all right, Susan. Don't be ridiculous. If anything were wrong, I would know.'

'But have you noticed how pale she is? A bit anaemic maybe. My friend Lynn was anaemic and she looked just like Nicola, her face so white it was kind of blue sometimes.'

'Nicola has delicate colouring. Not everyone is ruddy-faced, you know.'

Susan was attempting to stuff the turkey, but most of what was meant to go inside it was dropping to the floor. In disgust I pushed her away and took over; this ended her reflections on Nicola's health.

The person in question had in fact said how well she felt, and her gaze was more focused than usual, somewhat determined;

resolved to get through the day and the tasks at hand.

When she came back and saw I had done the turkey she sighed with relief. 'Oh, thank goodness, it's the meat, you know, I really cannot bear . . .' And she lit a secret cigarette – checking first that Augustus was not around – as if recovering from this task she had not performed.

Christmas Eve dinner began very quietly. Scott, when he was not drinking, had slept during the day; like a bear in hibernation his level of awareness was low. Susan, I thought, hoped to keep it this way. Yet the prognosis was not hopeful: his eyes were red, the fleck taken over from grey, and his neck was corded with the sort of innate tension which makes people grind their teeth in their sleep. He was half-asleep yet fully defensive.

Nicola was dressed in a way I had not seen before: nearly elegant. Instead of her usual gypsy cast-offs, she was wearing a close fitting black velvet dress which, although it made her look too thin, reminded me of the sort of thing Mother used to wear, not so much in style as in the sleek effect of it. That reedy slimness was unbreakable, tough. Nothing had ever defeated Mother – and Nicola? She appeared compliant, easy, mild; yet when had I ever observed her do anything she did not wish to do? People depended on her (her mother, her husband, now me) and though she hardly appeared able to sustain the burden yet she did, and with firm determination never to rely in return.

Though she does, I thought suddenly, rely on me to a certain extent, or for something in particular. Just as she once relied on Mother.

She was wearing make-up which I had never noticed on her before. Not just the usual violet eyeshadow, but rouge and bright red lipstick. The effect was dramatic, slightly bizarre, for she lacked the vitality to sustain such colour – though Mother was pale and wore red it somehow picked out the blood behind the skin, whereas on Nicola it merely pointed out the absence of it. I was reminded of make-up on old women, faking life when none was there, and wondered why Nicola did it – curious that artists could be so inartistic with themselves. I thought that, in a perverse way, Nicola with her new dress and unflattering paint was flaunting something, exhibiting some aspect of herself she normally kept hidden.

The roast was carved and served, wine poured – and being consumed all too rapidly by Susan and Scott – when Augustus turned to Nicola and said,

'Darling, I shall have to go into the hospital tomorrow. Mrs Watson is having her operation. I finally persuaded her to accept a gastrojejunostomy.'

'Really? I thought that . . . and, after all, the relief it will bring is only temporary and . . .'

But then her manner changed, abruptly, without warning. She leaned back in her chair and her voice became specific, penetrating, not at all vague. 'Tell me, Augustus, just why did you take it upon yourself to bully her into accepting something she had clearly indicated she did not want done to her?'

He was startled by her tone of voice; embarrassed.

Her face in profile, tilted and haughty, she repeated: 'Why, Augustus? What made you think you had the right?'

'Of course I had the right, darling. I'm her doctor.'

'Doctors are not gods, you know . . . however much you might think you know your patients as "whole people" you cannot know what it's like to be them . . . you cannot live in their place, or die in it . . .'

'Well, Nicola, be that as it may.' He was becoming impatient, not prepared to repeat the brief argument of a few days earlier. His small eyes like irritable rodents searched out Susan. 'More wine?' She looked round at him coyly, passed him a pink, passive smile which seemed to have instant restorative powers. His frown cleared, he beamed at the company while he poured energetically great gushes of wine into Susan's out-held glass. 'Anyone else?'

'What I am saying, Augustus, is . . . you have no right at all not to let people die if they so wish and as they wish.'

His quick glance said: must you? Must you do this in public?

She must; she could not do it in private. 'Your notion of healing is selfish . . . you do it only for yourself and you cannot bear defeat . . . you think every patient owes it to you to survive indefinitely, however dreadful the circumstances . . . you need the personal justification of medical success the way a . . . vampire needs blood.'

I laughed. 'Physician heal thyself.'

Augustus shifted back in his chair and peered myopically at me with something less than liking; then at Nicola in a curiously imploring fashion: surely she could not mean what she said. It was the strain of Christmas, that was all; women often behaved badly at Christmas. She knew the duty which lay behind her power over him; despite all appearances to the contrary, his life depended upon her approval, if she denied him as doctor he was nothing.

But Nicola was stronger than duty, she was private; her life, and her death, in the end were her own. She rose from the table and sailed towards the kitchen, looking as she went quite her usual wafting self, as if the argument were over, finished, forgotten. But I knew differently. I could tell she was angry. There was something just slightly brittle about her face, the edges had gone sharp though no one else would notice. I thought: Mother was this way when hanging onto rage. It will burst, she will never keep it back. Like the weather, so close and oppressive and cold; but weather, on the other hand, can forestall storms indefinitely.

Anyway, I thought, she has said the worst thing she can say to him. She will have to be careful now, stand back, stay away.

Scott was obviously inebriated by the time the dessert was served. The few words he said came out slurred and his eyes were tiny shark's eyes, dense and cruel. (I decided that the tattoo on his chest was a shark; there were serrated edges reaching for his throat which looked like fish teeth.) The redder his face became, the darker his hair plastered down like oily duck feathers on his bullet-shaped head.

When Augustus made to pour him a glass of dessert wine, I intervened.

'Shouldn't think that's wise, do you?'

Scott's head shot up. 'Guess I'm a better judge of that than you.'

'I wouldn't be so sure. But still.'

He turned to Susan and said loudly, 'What the sam-hell is wrong with your mother? She thinks she's real important, thinks she's got some goddam right to boss people about.'

Susan hiccuped nervously. 'It's just her way, that's all. Mom's English and it's kind of natural here, the way she behaves. Isn't it, Gus?' (But he seemed not to hear her.)

'Well, it sure as hell ain't natural to me.'

I decided to tackle him though there was hardly much sport to it. 'What *is* natural to you, Scott? Shooting things? A good fight in a bar? There are people for whom all that is not entirely natural behaviour.'

'Seems to me it's natural to show a little respect to people. Including next of kin, like daughters.'

'Oh, and have you got any? Daughters, I mean? Don't ask me why, but I can't say I've pictured you as the family type. What about parents?'

Susan tried to intervene. She squeaked out warningly, 'Mom, please . . .'

'Your parents must be disappointed not to have you with them this Christmas, Scott. Where do they live?'

'Mom, Scottie's parents aren't . . .' She paused anxiously, and glanced at him. 'I mean, they're not with us any more.'

'Not in prison, I hope.'

With this Scott began rising from the table. I was already bored, I could see the end before it came as if this scene had happened far too many times before. And I suppose it had.

127

Susan, trying to hold him back, attempted to explain what she knew ought not to be said. 'Mom, you don't understand. Scott's folks are dead, it was some kind of shooting accident.'

'Accident?'

Scott exploded, the veins in his forehead about to burst through the skin. 'Jesus, people sure as hell don't let themselves get shot on purpose.'

Nicola appeared with a bowl of whipped cream. How much of the exchange she had heard was hard to tell by her random contribution. 'Sometimes they do, you know, when they feel they have nothing to live for . . . or nobody worth living for, then it's revenge, of course, or punishment of some kind, and . . . Christmas is the suicide season, isn't it, Augustus?'

As if he judged her no more than an innocent vehicle of attack, Scott did not look at Nicola as he threw down his napkin. He raised one hand slightly, then let it drop uselessly. 'Suicide. Like hell.'

But his face looked shot. With unerring aim Nicola had taken him down as I never could. Colour drained from his face, his tattoo became a schoolboy's ink blotch, he shrank to the age he had been when someone came to tell him, or he found them dead. Of course I knew about death, I had recognized his misery. But I felt no compassion as he stalked from the room nor remorse as I pictured him packing with blind angry fists.

We all knew he would leave at once.

Susan left the table to cry and Augustus went after her. I could hear her monotonous grief and complaints. 'Mom always does this, she was just the same with my husband Donnie.'

For my part I felt a sense of order to things. The proper order. Scott was gone, Augustus was with Susan, and I had Nicola. She made no move to call Augustus back or comfort Susan herself. We finished dessert as if nothing had happened, thinking our own thoughts or talking our own family language.

FOURTEEN

✿✿✿✿✿✿✿✿✿✿✿✿✿✿✿✿✿✿✿✿

When I came to say goodnight I found Nicola in the living room looking out through the black window at the blackness beyond relieved by few twinkling lights for a city landscape. There were playing fields on the other side of the river, Augustus had explained; hence the dark. In it, Nicola was the loneliest person alive as if she had absorbed my loneliness, and Mother's too – a family condition, this disease of acute singularity.

'I am sorry, darling, about all the upset. Absolutely frightful, but then what else could one expect from a man like that? Still, I dare say it might have been worse.'

In her black dress Nicola blended with the window pane so that when she turned to look at me, her white face seemed to float disembodied towards me. She did not appear to have heard, she seemed confused. Her thoughts were separate and far away.

'Darling, I think I shall say Merry Christmas to you now. Seems more appropriate last thing at night rather than first thing in the morning, don't ask me why.'

I was not particularly aware of what I was saying; only that I wished to draw her from the window, so much black upon black. Her ghostliness upset me.

'It's a pity that Matty isn't with us to . . .'

'Oh, I'm sure she is, darling. In spirit at least.'

I said this lightly to disguise the fact that momentarily it seemed true; I felt Mother's presence, I sensed her watching me from a distance as she had the morning I left home; she was watching us both. Was she willing us home?

'Have you thought about Mother's bungalow?' Nicola looked startled as if I had read her very thoughts – so that was where she looked to out of the window: her gaze went halfway round the world. 'What I mean is, darling, you will have to decide what to do with it. To sell it or keep it, for a start.'

Nicola slowly draped herself across the couch and when she stopped moving it seemed as if she might never move again. Her bracelets mourned with a funereal tinkle.

'You would like the house, Hermione, really. I would like you to see it and . . .'

There was an edge of excitement to her voice now as it came back to life; she was slightly fervent, the way people are with invitations which imply more than is said; which derive from obscure, half-formulated hopes. But she was tired, she hardly knew what she meant.

'We should go together,' I replied seriously and sat down beside her.

She glanced round at me, a weary sideways sweep. 'Would you come, really? I . . .'

'Just say when.'

And I meant it. I was ready to go anywhere with her. I wanted only to be with her while I could; my feelings were suddenly focused with passionate intensity. All that had happened this evening, and since we first met, was leading up to this – we hovered on the brink, I felt, like lovers about to exchange vows.

I embraced her tightly, as she had held me in the taxi the day I arrived. I heard her exhale as if I had driven all the breath from her, and yet it was a sigh of inexpressible relief. At last, she might have said, at long last. The words were on my lips: I love you. Clear but unspoken. I waited, long seconds passed.

Nicola put her hand over mine. 'You want her back so badly . . . I am sorry.'

'Don't be, darling. I have you.'

FIFTEEN

❦❦❦❦❦❦❦❦❦❦❦❦❦❦❦❦❦

On Christmas morning I rose early. I wanted to help Nicola, and in particular I wanted to be with her before anybody else. I dressed carefully in what I would wear for the rest of the day: a green cashmere dress and red coral necklace and earrings – all very festive and Christmas-like.

As I brushed my hair and rolled it up I found myself surprised at what I saw in the mirror. I knew what I looked like and yet I did not; I was startled by the hawk-like nose, the penetrating eyes, the arched and quizzical eyebrows. Even the way that I looked back at myself, head tilted, gaze challenging: had I always maintained such a haughty demeanour or was something changed? It was Mother in the mirror; Mother, exactly. She was the one with such cold, distant ways; but what strength lay behind it all, what marvellous, invincible strength! Mother was indomitable; so was I.

Did I accept my inheritance? My life had been spent in denying Mother, and yet, by perceiving the resemblance, it was as if the mirror cleared: I could see myself as I had never done before, I could describe myself. Whereas before I had been invisible, nothing, no more than a shadow of my own hatred; a disembodied, acrimonious voice.

This was Nicola's doing. Somehow, by seeing Mother in her, blood-line run rampant, I was now seeing her in myself. Or was it Nicola's own purposeful eyes, her motivated perception of me taking root? You want her back so badly, she had said; but the same was true of her – had she created me out of yearning, a phantom given body by grief? If so her magic worked by my connivance and secret acceptance that I had always been Mother and that the greater the distance between us the closer our minds.

And yet I was not there when she died.

Instead I was here with Nicola.

I went down the stairs, silent with the sleep of others, and found the kitchen still dark and inactive. Nicola was not up yet. I was pleased – I would make a breakfast for the two of us, surprise her; conjoined in the pleasure of eating we might enjoy a few quiet moments together before the bustle of the day began. Nicola needed to eat more (remember how thin her wrists) – to make sure she started the day well-nourished I made toast, found cheese, scrambled some eggs.

Yet these very activities activated anxiety about Nicola, as if each effort to make her healthy testified to the fact that she was not. I recalled the way she was the night before; when I held her in my arms there had been so little there, just a figment of a person, just breath without breathing. Even Susan was concerned about Nicola's health and yet I had deliberately ignored all clues. Suddenly I was panicked and filled with remorse – was there something wrong with her after all? Perhaps I might have helped had I been aware earlier.

The darkness amplified my worries and I became very anxious for her to appear. At the back of my mind lingered the harsh belief that awareness of misfortune always comes too late, not as premonition but as afterthought. If I was uneasy about Nicola my awareness would be a requiem not a summons to her side. 'Help', indeed: I had never helped anyone.

I laid out the breakfast and considered going up to her bedroom, calling out softly so as not to wake Augustus. Unused to anxiety and doubt, I paced irritably about the table watching my food getting cold. But still she was not down.

It was not until I had poured myself a cup of tea that I

noticed a folded note on the sideboard across from the table. There was no name on it so I picked it up, opened it.

To my surprise it was for Augustus from Nicola.

This did not prevent me reading it.

I have left, she had written.

(At once the paper turned malignant, mocking in foreknowledge; revelling in the pain it caused. The incomprehension which most people feel had no chance with a shock such as this and with me: I knew she had left. I had been left before.)

I have gone away and will never return, she wrote. Nor do I wish to be found, please remember that. I know this is sudden and brutal but believe me, darling, there is no other way. It is impossible for me to stay with you because what I want is the one thing you cannot give. Never mind, it is not your fault. Believe that I did love you; your love for me is evidence of that. And believe that what I have done is best for us both.

She had signed it 'yours, Nicola'. Yours? Whose? She was mine, the note was mine.

I refolded it tenderly and tucked it into my dress as close to my heart as it would go. Then, as if physically striken I doubled over in pain. Ah, the pain, such pain, there is nothing so unbearable as rejection. I tried to speak to myself, I said: you are going to suffer, you must be prepared.

But when had I ever suffered like this before? Methodically I thought back to try to find a parallel event – as if this might help, as if one might learn from experience. I thought about Olaf's death, and it was grey; I brought to mind Susan and felt nothing but bright frustration. But when I thought about Mother, recalled her constant absence and crushing rages, when I remembered in particular waiting for her to love me the day my father left and how she failed, how she turned away – then that was it, the total blackness, the high-pitched hum of desolation. Nicola had turned away from me. On the brink of love she had deserted, just as Mother did on that and every other close occasion.

Nicola had left me. Oh my darling, I called after her. I cannot, I cannot survive solitude again. To be so close and to lose you – my heart was racing, bursting. I am ill, I cried, and now my ill spirit will never be well; it sobbed through my veins, up and down, back and forth, while my heart beat faster and my eyes began to cloud.

I suffered next a curious displacement. I felt myself to be so totally alone that I was nothing. This feeling is usually for me a prelude to rage, like an epileptic's aura, but this time when fury came, instead of exploding outwards, it wormed inwards like a deadly parasite.

I hated myself. I could not forgive myself.

It is all your fault, I said. It always has been. You were born bad: you spoil, you destroy; you would ruin the world in your own ruined image.

Your fault that Mother never turned to you when she drove your father away. You wanted him gone, you wanted Mother to yourself, yet she never claimed you – and why should she embrace the child of a man she did not love? An ugly child marred by some secret deformity – a secret because it was hideous, or hideous because it was a secret; hardly matters which, your fault either way. Mother looked to you to beautify yourself but you never would. A lovely child would have earned her embrace, a child with open arms would have drawn her in. Yours were stiff and angry, desperate, corrupted with need. Which was also the secret thing, and not just yours but a composite of murmurous longings from voices half familiar, half strange.

You are a stranger, a foreigner, an isolate. Everyone has abandoned you and it is right that they should do so. After parents there was Olaf. Poor man, he lasted your icy, waspish ways for years until his heart gave out with relief; he left you by dying and I know he accepted with huge, sad gratitude this sudden way out. He might have survived had he wished it, he could have struggled at least and not gone at once, had you been worth living for. Susan, on the other hand, has left you by not leaving entirely; by always being there to illuminate the shattering ineptitude of your begrudged responsibility. Her love makes you lonely because you cannot return it, her proximity confirms irrelation.

While you, for your part, left the only person with whom you might have been related; you turned away from the first and last relationship in life. Mother died without you: you left as a thief in the morning with her grief and never returned, never put things right in time. Oh, how you condemned yourself by this cruel omission, condemned her and yourself into the bargain.

Small wonder Nicola left. What could she want with such a person as you?

There would be no second chances now. Quite ludicrous the very notion: love not done right the first time can never be correct. No such thing as reparation, no absolution and release.

All this way I had come, halfway home just to learn that the journey might never be completed. I was damned: Mother damned me. Your fault, I cried out, and now we will never be forgiven.

I was confused, befuddled when my thoughts ran out. Shell-shocked I wandered into the kitchen. Everything was prepared for lunch, I realized in the clear light of day – as if Nicola had stayed up all night making preparations for this festive meal she would not eat. The turkey was in the oven cooking at a low temperature. I pulled it out to baste and thought, she could not bear meat. Putting in the mince pies to bake I thought, she loved the smell of spices. Use of the past tense, so automatically done, only confirmed that Nicola was definitely gone.

A thudding noise down the stairs warned me of Augustus's approach. I tensed like a cornered animal, I was not ready for him yet he would impose his loud, inquisitive presence. Trained to ferret out malfunctioning, he would know at once that something was wrong. I was too much weakened for effective camouflage and vulnerable to what might follow; I might let him see the depth of my bereavement, indeed display it and say with dreadful hope and gratitude, please heal me – can't you bring back the dead? There was nothing a man like him would like more. What a victory, what a marvellous salve to ease the anguish of his own pain! But he had used too many sufferers to try to cure himself; I would not have it that way – which meant my only option was attack.

When his dressing-gowned figure came into view I said frostily, 'Can't think what you're doing downstairs so early. There's no room in the kitchen, you know, for unscheduled eaters or casual grazing.'

He peered at me sleepily, his small eyes particularly blind. 'Merry Christmas, Hermione. Have you seen Nicola?'

'So far I've seen nothing but the inside of the oven. Perfectly frightful, when you think about it, all the food we feel obliged to consume just to celebrate. Your stove can barely cope.'

He stood next to me looking confused. 'She wasn't in the bathroom and she's not here in the kitchen.'

I thought to myself: he knows. That is, he doesn't *know* yet but he realizes. Even Augustus had instincts and, though they had not given him the slightest warning during the months when she started to separate, the day she finally left, foreboding woke him early.

Why not tell him right away? Get it over with. There was grave impatience as well as malice in my haste. I wanted it finished, this bit of the business done – his claims, his very existence, were an intrusion on my grief.

'Nicola is not here. She has gone.'

'Gone? Gone where?'

He was thinking about shopping, a quick walk along the river, when all the while he knew what I meant, he was doing what most abandoned individuals do (and I could not) – trying to delay the message, twist it, deny it before it could hit home.

For a moment I thought, he loves her. Momentarily it seemed quite clear that there were all kinds of love and I felt pity for them, every one. But, lacking pity for myself, such compassion came undone: he needed her for reassurance and that was too selfish a motivation surely to dignify the name of love. He was beginning to annoy me.

'I don't know where Nicola has gone, but I do know that she will not be coming back. She has left you.'

He began to shiver at those particular words as if what he wore afforded scant protection. His blotchy skin became more mottled with red patches. Still he would try hard not to know what he knew.

'That's impossible. What are you saying, Hermione? You are joking – I know your caustic sense of humour. Not entirely kind, if I may say so.' He was trying to work himself up to anger, yet was far too afraid for that means of defence.

'Nicola has left you and will never be coming back.' I could see I would have to keep repeating the message as to a child hard-of-hearing and none too bright.

At last he had heard and believed. He sank down into a chair in front of the uneaten breakfast I had made for Nicola and suddenly his eyes were wild and despairing. He was coming apart, he was being killed by the knowledge; to be denied, rejected, cut his heart wide open while some terrible surgeon disconnected his brain. Nicola had been his life, but then I knew that, I had seen his healer's hand plead for blessing, seen her head bend and give.

'Why did she leave?'

'Because she did not love you.'

137

The note in my dress stayed there. It was mine, after all, not his. I would tell him the truth he deserved.

He seemed to struggle physically with what I had just said. For some moments he was silent and I knew it was emotions and not thoughts which held back speech. Eventually one word thrust its way out.

'Bitch.'

Was this for Nicola or me? Or both of us? Not quite what I would have expected of him though part, I dare say, of every man's vocabulary. I comprehended immediately which way the fragments of his heart were turning. He was aiming at hatred, pushing guilt away, blaming; grasping after the illusion of dignity by means of righteous indignation. The easy way out, but then I knew he was weak: our husbands always have been.

'Fool,' I commented. A single word of condemnation to match his.

Yet I was the one condemned. All my scorn and contempt, my denial of his very humanity, were no more than a ploy against self-loathing. Attacking him was a joy: each blow drew my blood, I was dripping, staggering, staining my life.

And to no good purpose – I was just as alone.

SIXTEEN

❦❦❦❦❦❦❦❦❦❦❦❦❦❦❦❦❦

At around nine, early for her, Susan teetered into the kitchen in a tight bright red dress and on spiky rhinestone-studded heels which bore the plump weight of her with some difficulty. 'Merry Christmas, Mom.' And, 'Hi, Gus.' Her fresh-faced greetings drew no response.

'Is anything wrong?'

'Oh, for heaven's sake, Susan.'

She flinched at my sharpness. I looked at her fixedly – could she not see that now was not the time to ask questions? Augustus was slumped in a chair by the fridge; I was making myself busy with food we would never eat. Words had been done with – yet here was Susan trotting out the obvious question with bland, keen insistence. It amazed me sometimes that a person as passive and moulding to others as she, could also be totally insensitive.

And yet she was not: she sensed already the magnitude of loss sustained; she remembered it, knew well the shape and feel of shock. She came up to me and her hands went out but she was grown beyond the illusory solace of skirts and holding hard. She touched my shoulder lightly.

I felt myself beginning to give way and said quickly, before I might say more: 'You may as well know right away. Nicola has left.' My voice was as cold as I could keep it.

'Left, Mom?' Hers was Augustus's reaction: the same total confusion and lack of belief, as if this one small event of liberation were the least likely act in the universe. As if Nicola's leaving undid all reliable connections.

If husbands are the last to know of their wives' discontentment, was I the last to know another story, about the ties that bind, the shared enjoyments and rituals which make marriages persist for a lifetime? Nicola and Augustus had lived together in reasonable harmony for nearly ten years; this was fact to Susan, and hard evidence of happiness, while I saw only flaws and shadows cast behind. Was I blind to the brightness of life in this and every other matter? The darkness of my personal vision oppressed me yet I clung to it.

'Mom, what do you mean, she's left?' Susan was bearing down anxiously; I realized I had not answered her the first time.

'Nicola has left Augustus.' No point in indicating personal loss.

'Mom, I'm so sorry.'

She took my hand and kissed it. Her lips on this part of me unaccustomed to affectionate contact were strong with devotion, with the powerful will to console. I wish it was me, she was saying; I wish it was me you had lost and not her. She knew I loved Nicola. But instead of jealousy – my heart base – she felt pure gladness, simply and innocently, that I had the joy of loving someone. Now she felt pure sorrow at the enormity of my loss.

But her sympathy must be shared, and it was large enough for many. 'Guess I better talk to Gus.'

She was taller as she left me and went over to where he sat. Her red hips and bosom were wide with generosity, specific in their understanding. 'I know,' I heard her say to him, 'I know what it's like, I really do. When Donnie left me I thought I'd never get out of bed again, let alone carry on living. Believe me, Gus, I know how you feel.'

I wondered momentarily if she was like this with friends – a comforter, an unofficial counsellor distributing advice and sympathy among the needy. I had only ever seen her as my burden; now the weight of it had shifted.

Her carrot-coloured hair no longer looked garish on its Christmassy red background; it was burnished, golden, glowing with the light of angel distances from what I had taught her and she could not learn. She was right not to be mine. That this revelation was not love undid her destination, the easing of my grief. But with Augustus she would be more successful.

In the meantime she was practical. To me she said, 'Are you sure, Mom, that Nicola's safe? I mean, do you know that she's left deliberately and not gone missing?'

'There was a note. Like the sort that suicides leave.'

'I still kind of wonder if she's all right, you know, and not wandering round somewhere ill. It did seem to me like there might be something wrong with her. Maybe we ought to check out the hospitals.' Susan was puzzling over something, dimly wrestling with some hitch in comprehension. She still could see no reason for Nicola leaving Augustus; and still she harped on her cousin being unwell.

This made me lose my temper – an exquisite relief: 'For God's sake, leave well enough alone, Susan.'

She left me alone then, in a calm and quiet shifting of priorities, and turned her attentions where they would be appreciated: Augustus waited for her. He sat like a retarded child, mute with dependency, and when she suggested he ought to get dressed he rose to obey her with mindless gratitude.

She went upstairs with him, as if he might not find the way, but not before saying to me in a quick aside, 'It'll be all right for you, Mom, I know it will in the end. You'll see Nicola again, I'm sure of that.'

Her emphasis had been on the 'you', meaning that the same could not be said for Augustus.

In the days which followed, up until my departure, I saw a side of Augustus I would never have believed existed. He was nothing to me now that Nicola was gone, I felt no animosity and observed his new behaviour with an objective and indifferent eye.

Nicola's leaving undid him. Like a torn sweater his life unravelled before my very eyes. If he was worth abandoning, he had no worth; for several days he sat in a chair looking out at the river, unable to justify the slightest movement. His excuse for existing had been the healing of others; yet Nicola had found sickness in their marriage, a hidden pathology he never spotted though she, it would seem, was dying of it. What sort of doctor was he then?

He cancelled clinics, withdrew from a conference.

When he left the window he railed against Nicola. What sort of patient was she to have hidden all her symptoms? Not told him a thing. Had she ever committed herself to his loving care? There was pretence in her half-lidded wandering gaze; when she smiled it was a half-smile, when she talked her unfinished sentences hid volumes of meaning she owed him.

Susan listened patiently, nodding without confirming his resentful reconstruction of ten years' wedded bliss. And they had been happy years, that was the frantic, humiliating truth; happy at least for him. Susan fed him turkey and stuffing while he gobbled her attention; bits of cranberry sauce, like tawdry Christmas decorations, adhered to his once hygienic beard.

Late at night – I could not sleep – Susan talked to me about Augustus. She had gleaned more details of his past than I would ever have been bothered with, but I doubted that any of it had been told her directly; she simply listened carefully, sorted facts later, and deduced certain things from what he had not said. Uneasily I thought: if she can read so much about him, what truths has she secretly always known about me?

Apparently Augustus was an orphan, brought up by his great-aunt who was too old in spirit and in health for parenthood of any sort. She was constantly ill, he was constantly tending to her but totally without success. Begin a failed doctor, end a failed doctor: the two women in his life had refused to respond to treatment – were his hospital patients mere substitutes in an on-going effort to be allowed to succeed?

'He's a sick man, honey,' I said without sympathy but without rancour either.

An invalid finally, it would seem he had been one all his life. Dispensing care rigorously, insistently, endlessly, he had all the while yearned to be cared for in return. Susan was doing just this with consummate skill and sympathy he judged to be his own.

'He's grieving,' she told me.

'Nonsense. He's peeved. His pride is hurt.' I was the one who grieved; no one else had the right to that description.

Susan went about the house in jeans and stockinged feet. Without high heels, she was tiny like a well-fed mouse, like a chubby child who will never grow up. Unshod she moved with speed and deftness up and down stairs, between me and Augustus. I had the feeling of her watching over me even when we were not together. Had she not always done this, I wondered? Were her weekly visits, her failure ever to leave me, for my sake and not hers? A lifetime's assumptions can flip over in a moment; I felt the frailty of all my truths.

I noticed that she wore a man's cardigan which must have belonged to Augustus, and this reminded me of how she coveted Olaf's cast-offs as a child: wearing his sweaters was like wearing his love. Certainly she treated Augustus with all the care and attention she had shown to her father. She appreciates men, I thought, she takes to them naturally; feels more at ease in male company. It's the first love, I thought, it's her first love repeating.

I soon realized how she came by the cardigan. Susan was spending the night in Augustus's room. I was hardly surprised, she was generous with her sympathy.

In fact, the arrangement seemed entirely right and proper. I imagined how Nicola would be pleased. I thought: she wanted this, she knew. We both knew. The foreseeing of it allowed her to leave Augustus in the knowledge that he would not be left alone.

When Augustus began to rouse himself noticeably – the day before my flight back – his first activities were hardly normal. He burned all of Nicola's artwork he could lay his hands on; then spent the afternoon at the Tate Gallery in some vain hope that he might find her there planning more. Such magic never works. I, on the other hand, did exactly what I always do – wrote a little, read a little, cleaned the house. I missed my dogs.

Of course, this was no more therapeutic than Augustus's absurd antics. I felt that I had aged a hundred years. In the mirror I saw an old woman afraid of death. My white hair seemed yellow as if stained with nicotine; my eyes looked withered, mouth shrunk. The transition begun with Mother's death was completed by Nicola's desertion: I was finally in the last stage of my life.

Such an aged hag hardly deserved special care, and I was sloppy about dress for the first time in my life. No one else might notice lack of attention to detail, to small facts of grooming, but I did and degraded myself on purpose though without purpose.

I was expecting as much when Susan told me she would not be coming back to Montana. Just as well you have an open ticket, I said (congratulations hardly seemed in order). To me was given the task of arranging for her boys to join her. I shrugged.

Only from sheer habit did I question her later. 'Are you sure you should stay? Can Augustus take two small boys? I must say, it's hard to imagine water pistols and pet tadpoles in this house. But still.'

She beamed at me, pink lips sparkling with gloss. 'Gus always wanted kids. Anyhow he'll like my boys 'cause he really likes me.'

'That's what you say about all your boyfriends.'

'Gus is different, I know he is. Guess he feels I'll never hurt him like Nicola did. I've not ever left anyone, you know that, Mom.' She thought a bit, then added, 'Gus needs that much safety, like Scottie did.'

'And what do you get out of it all?'

'Kindness, Mom. Gus reminds me a bit of Dad.'

'God knows why.'

Finally the cold, fatal freedom from responsibility – I had wanted it, contrived its happening; yet now that it was true I dreaded the absence of disharmony ahead. A bad daughter is better than none: why had I not known this before?

Going back alone I flew into the night.

SEVENTEEN

❧❧❧❧❧❧❧❧❧❧❧❧❧❧❧❧❧❧

The only good thing about getting home was the dogs. Shelley was overjoyed to see me and the strength of her dumb, instinctive emotions momentarily stilled my thoughts. I knelt down and buried my face in her short fur, the way I used to do with pets when I was a child. As a temporary cure for despair this has always worked well; animals capture the present, distil it free of memory and expectation, until all that matters is what exists at that instant: warmth, softness, the resonant heartbeat.

Muriel came to the door soon after I got in after fetching the dogs from Rick's ranch. She held homecoming gifts: an apple pie, a rather sordid beef stew.

'I knew you'd be real tired, Mrs Tollefson, after all that travelling. Gosh, last time Bill and me went to Pittsburg I was knocked for a loop for a week. Just make sure you eat something, Mrs Tollefson. At your age it's real important.'

Since when had my age been her business? Was I looking as old as I felt? 'How was Christmas?'

'Real busy. You know what it's like, always cooking something, never stops. Jessie and Bill Junior came up from California. Said they was sorry to miss you.' She edged away from the dogs who were sniffing the air in the vicinity of her stew. Good idea, I thought: dogs' dinner. 'Say, how was your Christmas? It sure must have been exciting.'

'Perfectly marvellous.' She missed my tone of voice; accent always foxes her – she never hears me properly.

'Well, I'm real glad for you, Mrs Tollefson, real glad. And by the way, Bill shovelled your snow for you yesterday. Sure was a lot of it. We were afraid you might never make it to your front door.' She laughed. She wanted something: praise, a present.

Previously I would have discovered a sarcasm poised pertly on the tip of my tongue. But suddenly I lacked the energy, couldn't care less; said goodbye abruptly. Whatever it was that drew Muriel to me, and we had been in regular contact of one sort or another for ten years – none of it mattered any more. The pleasures of contempt had finally faded, and I knew that my indifference would breed indifference: this woman would soon begin to leave me alone.

For a while momentum kept me going. I phoned Donnie in Denver, made arrangements with him for the boys to journey out to London (at my expense, of course). I found him calm, reasonable, nearly intelligent; not at all the man I used to batter at blindly with scathing, disparaging comments. All animosity was gone between us – was it me, was it him? Or the simple fact that Susan was finally beyond his reach and that of all men like him? I was not very interested.

I went down to Big Timber to arrange for Susan's caravan to be sold. Strange that she had chosen to live this way, I thought, when I had offered many times to buy her and the children a house. Yet she was always somehow independent within my sphere of irritable concern; she kept her own counsel, her own ways, with a tenacity totally unaccounted for by her eager malleability in matters of love. Previously I had seen this side of her as signifying nothing but rejection of myself. Yet it was strength – and in that she was my daughter. Too late now to know it: the information was no longer of use.

I had never been inside her caravan. It was a jumble, as I would have expected, yet there was integrity of sorts, an order to it although I would never see it. She had been managing her own life despite my frequent interventions, and would continue to do so without them.

*

147

Managing myself was the problem, though not precisely a problem because I hardly cared to find a solution. I had lost interest in my own life, the way people can suddenly fall out of love, and there seemed hardly any point to seeing it through – how much longer, ten years, fifteen? – yet less point in the dramatic move of ending it. I hardly deserved suicide.

I endured being. Were I asked to define hell, I would have said it was immortality.

There was no longer any purpose to anything. I hardly went out; stopped riding at Rick's ranch, shopped once every two weeks for the dogs, not myself. I hardly bothered to eat, didn't dress unless I had to go to the supermarket. I packed away my jewellery and good watches for Susan the way old women do when death looks in the window. I was beckoning death, suggesting it hurry its claim on me.

I stopped writing. What point, when Mother would never read what I wrote.

I accepted finally that Mother was dead and gone. With the loss of Nicola I knew that I would never find her again. There would be no reunion, reconciliation; no starting anew. I would never have what other people call a mother and know, in this way, what was love – that fundamental thing which binds, a right, and the substance of all our small, peculiar lives. First things first: we must learn attachment from the cradle or it is never learnt at all.

Never was my lot. Not ever.

And yet sometimes I daydreamed the opposite story. As if defeat automatically breeds illusions of gain, I saw myself, a small child, back at Naivasha, sitting on Mother's lap and laughing (she passes me the binoculars, shows me where to look). Or I saw myself at Njoro walking across the lawn hand in hand with Mother to find the wounded bird Dr English invented. Sometimes we rode together, bridle to bridle, into the dark bearded forest. Once I conjured up a face which was Mother very old –

my face – and I rolled back the mosquito net about her bed, sat down, and tried to catch the slow inaudible words she spoke. But when I reached out to touch her red fingernails, to feel how smooth and young they were still, then her old voice said quite clearly, 'the ducklings have hatched,' which were exquisite words of love known to no one but ourselves.

With such thoughts I was trying to be mad. I wished for the solace of Mother's temporary escape – some small mental lapse during which my imaginings would stay real without conscious effort. No such thing occurred. Psychosis, unfortunately, was just beyond my reach. Not only was my blood count quite normal but I lacked the passion to go mad; emotion was drained out of me, I was purely cerebral.

I carefully considered the past few months. From a long way away I saw my foolish, panic-striken antics when news of Mother's death arrived. Avoidance and denial had been my full preoccupation: I would not have her dead, I would have Nicola instead. Small good my manipulations did me – in the end I found nothing but my own lack of worth.

Mid-February, on one of the coldest days that winter, temperatures around thirty below freezing, a telegram came from Dar es Salaam.

From the depths of my despair and certainty that Nicola was lost to me for ever, I was nonetheless unsurprised. I had been waiting.

The look of it was the same as the one in November. And the message? Not death, please not death again.

But Nicola was alive – maybe well – and living in Mother's bungalow by the sea. She asked me to come. Stop. Very important. No need to say more, she knew the briefest invitation would unhinge me, dislodge me. My tears blurred the words, splattered down and made splodges. When I spread the paper out on the counter to dry, Shelley at my feet whined disconsolately.

149

EIGHTEEN

❧❧❧❧❧❧❧❧❧❧❧❧❧❧❧❧❧❧

All the way out to Dar es Salaam I thought about Nicola. The telegram ran like a riddle through my mind: it was the things it did not say I wanted to know. How was she? In what manner was she living? What had happened between Christmas Eve and the present? That time lapse was a void, a yawning chasm I skirted in my mind, round and round I went, obsessively seeking some light to see by when the thing was in darkness, best avoided, better forgotten. As deserts and jungles flew past below me I was wild with excitement, elated, triumphant, yet without knowing why I felt dread and apprehension too, as if what I always wanted had never been my plan.

The plane sliced down through thick cloud towards my unknown home. This place which was nearly my birthplace and to which Mother had taken our home – which was herself, the atmosphere she created, and possessions which held the history of my childhood. So many years it took for me to arrive; as nothing, those years, I might have just left home with Mother watching, waiting to take me back. I thought about Nicola down below at the airport, looking up at the silver shape which bore me to them both.

It was raining. Not the gentle English rain at Christmas nor the healthy downpours of Montana, but a tremendous, drowning deluge which flooded the tarmac and tore leaves off the trees. I had brought an umbrella which quailed at the task, drooped under pressure and funnelled torrents down my legs. By the time I reached the terminal two-thirds of me was soaked. It will shrink, I cursed, my linen suit cannot stand water and my Gucci shoes will be spoiled. Yet it seemed right to pay some price. This was a spiritual pilgrimage which would ruin or redeem me. I was close to tears again, an unusual condition but one which had plagued me since Nicola's summons.

Weakness made me sharp and irritable, abrasive. There was a long queue through immigration and health, which hardly improved my temper. Nor that of my fellow travellers. A West African in robes ahead of me fell into an argument with the *polisi* examining his vaccination records. I asked the man ahead of me, an Asian, *'Kwa nini matata?'*

He answered in English with a less than friendly look. 'He has not been revaccinated for cholera. We have to be careful. There is an epidemic at the moment. Most schools are closed.'

'How perfectly frightful. I dare say everything else is closed too. Any excuse for a holiday.'

He wriggled his head and looked away.

Customs when I finally reached them were not much interested in me, having done well in bribes and confiscations from earlier passengers.

'Sina kitu cha kulipisha ushuru,' I said frostily.

The official smiled broadly – perhaps at my Swahili – and waved me through. *'Kwaheri, Mama.'* I was taken aback: since when had white women been 'Mama' and not 'Memsabu'? I sensed, not disrespect, but friendly indifference. He's but a boy, I thought, he cannot remember white rule.

Released into the country, I experienced a moment's panic in the large concrete hall without. I could not see Nicola. All confidence crumpled, anticipation turned to dread – after all I had lost her before, she had vanished when I was most sure of her; might not she do it again? Where was she?

But a white form like a Halloween ghost, more a moving sheet than a person, was winding its way through the crowd towards me. Faceless, it wore a floppy-brimmed hat and waved a stick-like hand. I dropped my suitcase and dashed.

Our first embrace was bliss. It told me everything, and that I was everything to her: she needed me as much as I needed to love her. My devotion was not only intact but stronger than ever, a tremendous force. With childish simplicity I thought to myself, all is well now, everything will be perfect. My life had been worth bearing so long just for this.

'Darling, how are you?' Still I could hardly see her beneath the hat.

She bypassed the question with: 'Super to . . . oh, I . . . marvellous, so good . . . come anyway.' Her words quivered and dipped in the air like damaged butterflies.

For the first time ever I found her quite incoherent. Her words were lost notions: the tenuous, delicate linkage hesitation previously sustained had come apart, been stretched too far. If she could not communicate, could she think?

She murmured on as we progressed towards the door. 'The rain, you . . . super umbrella . . . so exhausting for . . . a very long . . .'

I went cold with the effort of listening, cold with fear. She reminded me of people whose brains have been hurt, the way they try so hard to talk, and the more they try the less sense they make. It was as if finally she wanted to tell everything, complete each sentence, but the words which fell out, instead of meaning her life, were an idiot's mumble.

It was rather like coming to someone only to realize they are blind and can no longer see you, or mad, and can no longer know you. How would we talk if Nicola lacked both vocabulary and syntax? I had never talked to anyone as I had to her at Christmas, and there was more to be said, I needed her speaking.

It's the excitement, I decided. And to a certain extent I was right. As my apprehension faded I began to understand her.

Like a tap turned off, the rain was gone when we stepped outside. Humidity was fierce, steam rose from the road; I could hardly breathe in the heat and the moisture, I wiped at perspiration which would never evaporate. Nicola gave instructions to a taxi driver and we clambered into the musty interior of his car.

Another drive back from another airport: there were simple patterns to our connection, simple and sweet repetitions. But I willed our story onwards – and so, I believe, did she.

In the confined space of the taxi, Nicola removed her hat. I was shocked by what I saw. She had cut her hair; all gone the long dark braid, and in its place short, awkward strands which were scarred with grey (the silver threads from Christmas had multiplied like weeds). Yet I could see why she did it, her neck was so thin, it could hardly support the head above let alone a trailing weight of heavy hair. Nonetheless I mourned; my hair had never been cut, nor had Mother's. 'Darling . . .' I could not finish.

Then I looked at her face. It was emaciated, skin drawn tight across bone so that the essence of her showed, the humps and hollows of her skull. Her nose looked fractured, a jagged piece of bone, no longer delicate but detrimental, inherited damage without the amiable cladding of flesh. When she looked round at me, returned my gaze, her eyes seemed bleached – by the sun perhaps – to a paler shade of blue, more intense and glittering. She put her hand over mine but the arm behind it was desiccated, a mere twig of a limb; scant reassurance that all was well. Her half-smile still hovered but as a mockery of what she used to be, and still was, but in exaggerated form the way shrunken heads preserve the main features largely while all else is diminished. The softness, the moistness, the movement of her was gone. Her parchment eyelids, more half-shut than half-open, drooped in a mournful farewell.

'Nicola, what is the matter with you?' It came out as a cry. I heard it before I knew I had said it.

She ran her fingers through her hair taking clumps of it out like old grass. She took a deep, last breath.

'I am dying, Hermione.'

*

No hesitations: a message smooth and clear of interruption. The easiest thing in the world for her to say, when all else was terrible effort.

'Dying?' I repeated.

Outside we were passing a shantytown with tin roofs and open drains. Lepers lacking toes and fingers begged with stumps by the side of the road. Were they dying?

Nicola's head nodded like an empty pod. The world was dying – what did her small part in it matter? Suddenly indifferent, her attention wandered here and there, inside and outside of the vehicle, as if what she had just told me were of no consequence whatsoever. She had said the worst thing she could say, then forgotten it.

It seemed to me then that I had always known Nicola was dying; known but refused what I knew. When I planned the trip to London, that sudden and driven decision, was it not intuition, a long distance message that Nicola was gravely ill and I must see her soon or never? Perhaps the day she knew was the day I phoned. I had seen death the moment I spotted Nicola at Heathrow, and every day thereafter the clues had been ample and obvious – the thinness, the pallor, the shivering, the fatigue – I had seen yet preferred to remain blind.

Avoidance. Surely there was power in it. Deny the devil and he ceases to exist. 'What exactly do you mean, Nicola? Dying of thirst? Dying from the heat? Everyone finds the coastal climate trying. Don't you have air-conditioning?'

'I have cancer, Hermione.'

Blackness began to close in on me; panic and dread. She was leaving me again, slipping away to a place where I could never join her. What sort of cruelty was this, to bring me back as witness to her final departure? It was punishment and a dreadful one, the ultimate act of exclusion.

Anger erupted like a child's terrified scream. 'How dare you! How dare you bring me all this way for . . . this. Why?'

'Because I am . . . frightened, Hermione, I . . .'

The fear of us both fused together, we fell together. All the loss I had ever known began to surge from me in tears which could not flow as fast as their source provided grief. Loss and deprivation, the tremendous fear of being alone, held us together in the tightest embrace.

'How long?' I whispered.

'A few months . . . perhaps . . .'

I stroked her head and the sad wisps of hair which clung to my hand with useless static.

Silently I said a prayer: Mother, I said, please help me.

NINETEEN

❦❦❦❦❦❦❦❦❦❦❦❦❦❦❦❦❦❦❦

For a week or so Nicola and I said little of consequence to each other. It was the aftermath of shock, the automatic numbing that follows such a blow.

I realized that everything I had felt, Nicola felt too. My horror and despair at what she told me revived her own when the news was first broken to her by a doctor in November. Telling me – no one else knew – made it definite once again, her inexorable fate, not some self-tormenting fancy of a masochistic mind. Unavoidable, inevitable: a condition of the body without mercy. Now that I knew, she knew beyond the slightest trace of dream-like doubt.

Because, she explained, '. . . at Christmas I felt rather distanced, you know, not real . . . feet not quite on the . . . almost euphoric sometimes, as if my secret were marvellous news and not . . . they say bereavement sometimes works that way.'

Truth spoken allowed the disease a tighter grip and Nicola's condition worsened. She was no longer floating, shivering and pale; reality was harsh – she was in pain.

'To be expected, I . . .' She took to her bed.

. Mother's bed. Though the mattress was a new one, of course, as the original had been damaged by fire when she died. Snowy-white mosquito netting hung down from a frame, like a shroud, like a gigantic butterfly net fixed in place to stop souls from escaping. (I suffered from the strange delusion that if Nicola slept unenshrouded I would surely find her lifeless in the morning – so strongly did I feel sometimes that her spirit, or some part of her, was bent on premature departure.)

One tends to think of the dying as travellers preparing for their longest journey, all thoughts ahead with none for those left behind; one imagines that the pain of parting is totally one-sided and the burden of the bereaved. Not so: Nicola was struggling with the proximity of loss as much as I was. That a moment was soon approaching after which she would never see me again was as frightening and intolerable for her as life alone was for me. Indeed, I think it seemed to Nicola that she was the one being left behind, or forced to disembark, while I was the traveller continuing downstream.

She liked me to sit with her, even if we sat in silence, in order not to waste the time left us. Sometimes she talked about her past; gave me brief spasms of explanation, random bits and pieces which I fitted together later and then threw the whole away. What, after all, did I care about her life with Augustus, her reasons for leaving him?

She said, 'I began as his patient, you see, so my death would have been the worst thing I could do to him . . . a terrible denial of his skills and aspirations.'

What she wished me to grasp, and I tried to avoid, was the great difficulty she experienced in leaving him. The way they were had worked, she had played her role quite happily and willingly until her illness. Yet when it came to death their union lost validity: born alone, one dies alone – her demise was her own, she would design it as she wished. It was, in the end, for her sake and not his that she left. She wanted clarity; peace and privacy rather than the clamouring of medical intervention; dignity up to the final moment in place of helpless fear and dependency.

She said she had always felt determined not to die the way Angela did.

Yet she had summoned me, she was not alone; she needed my presence. She had come home to die – was I merely Mother's substitute? Undoubtedly I stood in for that person who had been a source of courage and inspiration when she was young, but perhaps there was more. Some service only I might perform for her. Tell me what it is, I thought; just tell me. There was nothing in the world I would not do for her.

As it was, I ran the house. This came to me easily, the dealing with servants, giving orders, checking on performance. The houseboy Husseini was new, hired by Kumar, Mother's solicitor, just before Nicola's arrival. She had never broken him in correctly: he was slow, lazy, lackadaisical before my firm hand descended to correct his ways. For several days I trailed him round the house, criticizing, giving specific orders for improvement; after that I made spot checks to keep him on his toes. He cleaned in places he had never cleaned before, under couches, low tables and behind Mother's piano; he beat the rugs, polished the silver and brass, and dusted all the books. Then I had him air the linen which was starting to grow mould, and spray for cockroaches in the cupboards. The house was full of insects driven indoors by the rain; these were his to destroy, and when I found a mantis or warrior beetle in the living room I would call him at once: *'Dudu hapa. Fanya haraka!'* Coming, Memsabu: his fez clinging desperately to the back of his head he would appear on the run, armed with a broom and a can of insect spray.

I took on the garden which hardly deserved the name. Since Mother's death it had run to ruin, what there was of it, the sandy soil being inhospitable to all but a few plants. I had the shamba boy trim the bougainvillaea, plant marigolds, stake out the tomatoes running wild. Several coconut palms had grown branches overhanging the roof; these I ordered him to lop off.

And so I occupied myself as if nothing were wrong. Looking back it seems that I clung to myself – that is, my mind hung on tightly to the form of me going about daily tasks; watched with relief this unfeeling figure of busy normality. I suppose the capacity to know tragedy is limited; like concentration it comes and goes and flags from over-use.

Even Nicola seemed to forget the truth occasionally – I could tell from the way her eyes lit up, then faded again when she remembered. But we never spoke of dying again. What point?

TWENTY

❧❧❧❧❧❧❧❧❧❧❧❧❧❧❧❧❧

On the eve of my sixtieth birthday, nearly two weeks after my arrival, Nicola, who was feeling somewhat better, stayed up after dinner to join me for coffee on the verandah. The garden was damp and steamy, and the silence noisy with the croaking of frogs brought out by the rains; between the black silhouettes of palm trees could be seen the sea aglitter with moonlight. Nonetheless it was the dark of black velvet beneath the steep overhang of roof, and Husseini carried out to us a kerosene lamp by which to pour coffee and see each other's faces.

It brought out the hollows in Nicola's face so that she was composed more of shadow than light. Her speech was all shadows of words, dark sounds from a long way off – the distance from her mind to her mouth had become immense and burdensome. Yet in her own way she was cheerful, pleased simply to be and be here, enjoying the night in my company. When she wished, and was able, she could concentrate on the present moment far more intensely than people who are well, and she drained each moment of its every drop of interest, no wastage now that time was of the essence. And I for my part did not waste time seeing death in her; the devastating picture which assailed me at the airport had given way, now that I knew the truth, to positive imagery, to a composite portrait constructed of what she still was, not what she was not – and the shadows in her face were radiant decay.

The mosquitos were vicious – I lit a mosquito coil and placed it at our feet. Sitting up again I caught my arm against a pair of binoculars hung over the back of Nicola's chair. Had she put them there or were they never removed after Mother died?

'Those look frightfully old and decrepit. We once had a houseboy who used to say when he broke something, "its day had come" — and I would say the same of the wretched binoculars — somebody ought to drop them, put them out of their misery.'

I often found myself assuming an air of levity with Nicola: what point now in solemnity? And she laughed, whereas at Christmas there was only, and always, the stoic half-smile.

'I have to say that these binoculars do not have the best of associations for me. They make me feel excluded just looking at them — took so much of Mother's attention, they did.' I was still joking, chatting lightly. But then I slipped inadvertently into bitterness. 'They remind me of the day Mother drove my father away.'

'Your father? I . . .' Nicola sounded surprised.

'You know, Mother's first husband. Tom Goodenough, your grandfather.' There were times when I wondered how much Nicola's mind was affected by her condition; she had odd lapses of memory. I tried to restrain my quick irritation for on this one topic I was automatically abrupt.

'Oh, Hermione, you know, there is . . .' She paused, thought a moment. Lit a cigarette, inhaled deeply with her head thrown back. Her lifeless hair turned vibrant in a halo of flaming curls as the lamp-light caught it. 'There are things, Hermione . . . things you should . . . I had not realized, you see, that you did not know . . . it came as a shock to me at Christmas, your ignorance of . . . and I was not sure I had the right to tell you but . . . now it seems I have no right not to tell you because Matty would have wanted you to have the truth.'

It had cost her dearly to say this much — she looked exhausted already though she had only begun. I had no idea to what she was referring, this truth like some sort of an heirloom, but sensed its grave importance. My first instinct was to spring forwards, grab at what she offered me as mine, my knowledge, my birthright. I knew it was owing me yet dread dragged me back. Though it was also anger of some sort, a kind of petulance: why should I be so eager now for what no one would give me in the past? My revenge it might be to refuse, to deny.

'Let's not talk about the past, darling. Enough was said at Christmas. It's the present that matters to us now.'

And it was. I feared for the present, such a fragile and temporary construct. Unnecessary words might undo us, our trust, our attachment; truths that one can live without can often be destructive.

'For your sake, Hermione . . . it's true, you see, that knowledge is freedom, at least I think so, and Matty did, she . . . would have told you if you ever came home.'

Her breathy voice had hardened into shrill insistence, a curious desperation which would not be denied or avoided. She quivered with excruciating determination – when had I ever seen her this way, so driven, almost frantic? She would be heard: it was the privilege of the dying, my duty to listen.

'Very well, Nicola, what would she have told me?' There was, in the end, nothing I would not do for her. 'I want to know.'

But Nicola could never come straight to the point. She started some distance from the heart of the matter.

'You know that Matty was not . . . faithful to her husbands.'

'So I always suspected.'

'She had someone else, a long-term lover who was with her for many, many years and she . . . loved him.'

'I would not be too sure about the love. But still. Who was he?'

'Dr English.'

'What? Never! Anyone but him, darling. You must have got it wrong.'

'Not wrong, Hermione . . . she loved Dr English and he loved

162

her, well, it must have been so obvious, even when I met him it was obvious . . . yet you and Mummy never . . .'

'How do you mean "obvious"?' My patient amusement was strained, threatening to turn into hysterical laughter. Was black white and white black? Quite ludicrous, the very idea that the only man I never feared was a traitor in our midst, my rival.

'The way they were with each other . . . they talked and touched in such a . . . kind way, so hard to describe it, and then when he died she went to pieces, first time in her long, hard life . . . completely collapsed without him, I mean, the breakdown.'

Though I wanted no details she gave them to me reverently in broken fragments like precious porcelain somebody has smashed. They met, Mother and Dr English, when Angela was born; she had a particularly bad bout of malaria, he treated her. (This much I knew – with relief I thought, no, she can tell me nothing new. Yet I listened on restlessly, defensively alert for proof that her notion of love was misguided.) They took to each other gradually, so said Nicola – indeed everything in their history was gradual, slow-burning, long-lasting. There was no huge conflagration, just a low persistent flame. Cool in manner Mother was cool with love. They liked each other and that 'like' deepened of its own accord.

He was firm and steady unlike other men she knew; no extravagance, no promises. Indeed he was the only one in her experience who was totally loyal and reliable. (I could agree with that – though not with what followed.) How did Matty know he could be trusted? Nicola asked rhetorically; because he was married and would not leave his wife. She had stayed behind in England for reasons of health and there was never any question of divorce to marry Matty. (Certainly no question.)

Deception never works indefinitely. Tom Goodenough became suspicious of Dr English, and threatened that if Matty would not end the association he would take Angela and me away from her. Dr English or us was the real issue of their final quarrel on the morning of my birthday.

I had to correct her: 'Shouldn't think so, darling. The poor sod forgot my birthday. That was nearly as heinous a crime as forgetting Mother's.'

Nicola merely shook her head and continued. Other husbands were either imperceptive or tolerant, she said (or quite right to suspect nothing, I thought). In consequence, for years the affair continued, on and off, until Dr English's wife died and then Jock died. He and Mother met in Dar es Salaam but did not marry – no point now after all those separated years. Habits had been formed, they stayed neighbours, loving neighbours; an arrangement which suited them well.

Bald facts, these fragments, and what did they tell me? Little I did not know already except for the detail that they had enjoyed each other's company in later life. The difference between Nicola's version and mine all turned on the quality of friendship: we agreed it was close but was it carnal?

Nicola saw my complacent expression through the darkness. 'You don't want to know, Hermione, because you . . . don't know it all.'

'Is there more?'

I could not see her well because she had leaned back in her chair, but her intensity when she replied was like an electric current passing between us.

'Yes, oh yes . . . you see, he was your father . . . Dr English was your father, your natural father, I mean.'

I believed her. Even now I wonder how and why it was that I refused her tale of lovers yet accepted immediately this startling revelation which had never ever crossed my mind as a possibility.

I can only say that, this time, I recognized truth when I heard it. There is a crystal ring of familiarity to that which is real; I accepted what she told me because I had always known it, yet never known that the knowledge was there. Refused to know, but gave in finally – because of Nicola, because of the force of her insistence. Her onslaught was in the end irresistible. I must hear and receive her fact about my parentage, she allowed me no choice.

Retroactively I accepted the truth of all that Nicola had told me. Mother in love, Dr English my father: as if I were dying for a moment I saw my whole life clearly. Yet previously I had avoided her messages with cunning. Nicola as good as told me at Christmas – but I would not understand, I let her hesitations shield me from an explicit statement which might have insisted I finally let go.

Of what? Of hatred. The logic was so obvious, so pellucid and pure: if Mother loved my father, she loved me. Something broke inside, some gigantic dam of grief and dejection; she loved him, she loved me, she had always loved me.

I never knew that fathers were important – yet here was the connection, here the resolution. And without logic, in the end, only feeling; because there is no hard reason to a child's susceptibility and an adult's closed mind. Nicola's words were a magical rune which undid the self-styled curse, my cage: my hatred. Stepping free I gasped in reply, 'I love you,' and the past untied.

I was back at the beginning. Naivasha, my sixth birthday. I had always told myself the events of that morning from a child's-eye view which saw everything yet not enough, and from which I extrapolated an adult's judgement: she rejected me as the child of a man she rejected. Yet now, as if I had grown out of that scenario, the perspective was altered, the story not the same.

Mother is trying to defend me. She has always been defending me though her means has been cool reserve, a feigning of less than preference, to lead him away from his lack of responsibility towards me. 'Him', this man, her husband who is not to be trusted, has dragged her finally to a dreadful impasse: lover or children, he has said she must choose. An ultimatum unworthy of a gentleman, unworthy even of his jealousy and pain; he wants control, he knows if he can bend her now, she will always succumb to his will. So, at breakfast, he plays with her sense of entrapment, he is provocative and overbearing, confident in the outcome of their conflict.

He ought never to have involved her child. This tips the balance which was anyway against him. His unsubtle toying, drawing me in then displaying his indifference, infuriates Mother who decides to play her final card to keep me from him for ever.

Not your child, she says. Have I always known? Has he?

Leave us, she says to the man who is not my father. Leave us alone. Her possession of me and my inestimable value are ringingly implicit in her threatening cry. She is fighting for me, I am the reason for her fierce, indomitable stance. Because she loves me.

I wait to hear her say it. She has never said 'I love you'.

She gazes around blindly, still bloodied from conflict. She fumbles her memory for words, the right words. But habit and the heat of battle have undone her vocabulary – 'the ducklings have hatched,' she says, and searches wildly for my face, my eyes, as if eyes might receive it, what she wishes to tell: her love.

This time I hear.

This time I reply what I mean. I leap from my chair and dart over to where she stands by the steps. I wrap my arms around her, hold her tightly in an embrace so close that not even air can come between us.

'I love you, Mother. Please forgive me.'

Wonderful words, miraculous words, all grief dissolves. History rewound and erased, we might now start again to write a story of closeness instead of separation.

But Mother is old. I look down: the woman I hold is a frail, brittle creature, delicate beyond emotion in the arms of death. I can smell cigarettes and perfume, a sweet, narcotic mixture, and there is fire somewhere, I hear it, a crackling and cackling, and her cracked voice nearly reaches me through a lifetime's evasion with something which sounds like 'at last' or 'at least' or it might have been 'father' – a tremendous expression of relief and release. I sense evaporation, an exquisite extinction.

I repeat the only requiescat: 'I love and forgive you.'

But suddenly she is struggling. I am startled, shocked, astonished. Why? What was it?

It was Nicola in my arms. She was gasping for air, trying to call out my name. 'Hermione, Hermione, I can't . . .' Her face was a figment of my imagination, I gazed at her in horror and let go.

Then she fell.

Fell backwards down the steps. I hardly knew what had happened except that she was leaving. The next thing I was aware of was smoke; the lamp had caught on her dress and fallen with her. I darted down after her, stamped on the flames starting up at her skirt; knelt down beside her.

She was lying at a very odd angle with her head so far back that the neck must be broken. I knew she was broken, knew at once.

There were no words I could possibly say. I could not even touch what I had done. But she said, quite clearly, 'Oh super, and . . . how good of you to come.'

Then her eyes closed completely.

POSTSCRIPT

❧❧❧❧❧❧❧❧❧❧❧❧❧❧❧❧❧❧

I never doubted afterwards that Nicola had summoned me to kill her. She was afraid of the slow ending ahead of her – she had said so – and in particular afraid of losing control, the very thing she strove to avoid by leaving Augustus. If she knew that he would not let her die easily, she was equally sure I would hasten her death. And that was what she wanted, that was what I might do for her. An accident: my love was the sort to cause accidents, fatal chance events; by virtue of its morbid nature, dangerous because so much confused with hatred. I was driven, obsessed with Mother of whom Nicola was a clear reflection, a cherished stand-in. Just as I stood in as Mother for her, as that huge and responsible figure of her childhood and the only one ever who could help. Would Mother have killed her? A final coup de grâce?

With Nicola's death my childhood was over. The hatred, the yearning, and the speculation. She freed me with fact and in fantasy, the delusions of my gratitude. Through her, Mother died in my arms with my love and forgiveness and I would like to think that her spirit was released like a bird shooting upwards. A martyr, was Nicola, in a sense, for future generations of our mothers and daughters: Mother and I had to be corrected like a damaged link in a chain so that all future links should hold fast. We transmit, after all, we do as we have been done by.

Liberated, I nonetheless cannot claim to be more than semi-enlightened. I will never understand entirely the intricacies of my relationship with Mother – or with anyone else. Doubt will never fade entirely: the mother I held in my arms at the end was a dream mother, after all, with the flesh and blood of another; I said love and forgiveness, those necessary words of absolution, while she merely mumbled her own visions. There are still moments when I long for the real voice, the real face. Imagination is never quite enough, my mind is not Mother.

And knowing is not changing. Now that I have traced with words the patterns of illusion and delusion which shaped my life from one death to the next, though they have lost their power I nonetheless wear them with a certain pride. No one would think me changed and I hardly feel myself a wise or saintly stranger. I think about Mother, and Nicola, every day. Obsession is a hard habit, difficult to break – and I like to go through the motions of it which still tell me who I am.

I like my life as it is. I am at home, finally, here in my mother's house and country, and I live as I was always meant to live. The only thing to cloud my satisfaction is health, for it seems I have a serious heart condition. This was diagnosed nearly a year ago and has so far given me few problems except the compulsion to write our family history while I may.

Before breakfast I write; a pot of tea beside me, the shutters open to the cool early morning, the sea gently roaring in the background. Later I walk a long distance along the beach (Dr Mengai tells me exercise is good in moderation – I agree but prefer to walk to the point of fatigue). I buy fish from the fishermen, look in coral pools if the tide is out, and my black labrador Blake comes with me. What a treasure he is, the darling, dashing ahead, walking to heel, or lingering behind to dig for crabs.

Then lunch, then siesta. After which I swim and have tea. Over tea on the verandah I scan the surroundings for birds; I am beginning to know the migrations, what birds to expect when, though the perennial crows are my favourites, those huge, rude creatures which scream at the palm trees and the rain and my dog. The evenings are quiet and star-laden, and I think about those absent as I sit at the table set for one – despite which I always change for dinner, always. Last thing, in bed beneath the mosquito net I read my grandfather's poetry; but find nothing of Mother in it nor sense her reading with me: she let go of him when I let go of her.

I live in Mother's footsteps without precisely being her. Sometimes I think about Dr English who, after all, has been more precise to me than other men long before I knew our true connection; but it is far too late to call him Father. Indeed I cannot even call him 'my father', a term of reference always low in sentiment and still designating, for me, Mother's first husband. Well, what does it matter, what's in a name? I am too old to learn masculine nomenclature.

Susan came to visit me six months ago and brought her new baby. Oddly enough it was Augustus who suggested the trip (and financed it), and he seemed particularly keen that their infant daughter go too, as if little Helen personified proof that his transference of devotion from Nicola to Susan was complete. Well, I needed no confirmation of this – a man as deeply dependent on one woman as he will always find a substitute and as quickly as possible. Susan was not only an eminently suitable candidate but there when his need was the greatest.

I advised against bringing a baby, and I was right, of course. Susan arrived drained by a sleepless journey, then collapsed with flu, while poor Helen who had a heat rash screamed endlessly until Husseini's wife took over as ayah. Oddly enough, I did not mind any of this. I discovered the moment I met Susan at the airport that something was changed between us. I was relaxed, no longer irritable, and nothing she did seemed done against me.

There was an easy warmth and gladness between us such as I would never have expected. The tension was gone: I needed nothing from her.

Nor she from me. All she ever wanted was my peacefulness; in her own life she had always felt a certain smooth tranquillity through all that I called chaos. The guiding hand of her father, I suppose, never left her. She liked her life, feared for mine: I was the straggler, the rogue animal, not her. She knew she loved me and her only regret was for me, that I did not know I loved her.

Saintly, in a way, is Susan, if you catch her in a certain light. Otherwise she is generally pleasing. When I met her at the airport I saw an attractive woman – had marriage to Augustus changed her appearance? She was still wearing jeans and high heels; too much make-up. But her hair seemed more natural, less fixed into the wrong shape and so glorious a copper colour that I hoped little Helen (encumbered with her father's looks) would inherit it. Susan's round sturdy shape was agreeable and healthy, reassuring like the earth and as providing. She was maternal and I liked her; I could not help but like her. Her eyes seemed different; perhaps a change of make-up. I had always known they were brown but not that brown, so deep, so warm, so steady. Her grandfather's eyes: I saw that at once. My eyes too.

We talked a lot, Susan and I. Though I remembered us in silence, incommunicative, in fact I suppose we had always discussed matters of mutual concern in our own way. Were things ever as bad between us as I thought? She listened to me keenly and without apprehension because the old habit of swift retribution, cutting comments, disparaging looks, was gone from me, soaked out by the heat; no longer necessary.

Because I loved Mother I loved Susan: reconciled with the former I was released to the latter. I had a daughter finally, and a real one.

I wanted her to know it all, the reasons for the rift between Mother and me, the logic of its healing.

'From the beginning there were problems, honey. It was the secret that started it, the fact that she felt she must hide how much I meant to her, and why. After all, the child of a beloved must mean more than a child born without love.'

'I know you cared for Dad.'

I glanced at her, no reassurance required, then went on. 'I knew she loved me but could never find confirmation of it. My reasoning denied her true feelings and in the end I was forced to deny my own.'

'Faith helps.'

'I have never been faithful.'

'Sure you have, Mom.' (I waved this aside, impatient to continue while my thoughts were focused.)

'I was a difficult child. No point in denying that. And the more unpleasant I became, the more I let her down, the harder it was for Mother to try to put things right. She did try, you know, as best she could. Small things, small favours. But she felt helpless, hemmed in by habit. She never knew where she went wrong or what to do about it. I reminded her of her alcoholic father in the way I rejected her, my consistent bad behaviour – the only way she could explain it all was to say I was like him. At this point I suppose a vicious circle set in, and the more she expected disappointment, the more she got it.'

'I'm sorry, Mom.' A simple pause of recognition, then she added, 'But I guess Grandma kind of understood anyway what you really felt. Parents always do, deep down. Just like kids always know. It's the saying that tends to come out wrong, that's all. It's the words, not the heart.'

I laughed at the way Susan could be trite yet profound like the lyrics of some popular song. And why not? – the behaviour of people is never original.

'I never thought about fathers. There was only Mother and me. And yet I clung to a piece of bad logic: she had hated my father, therefore hated me. Well, she did hate the man that I thought was my father. But the point is, you see, that I knew the secret but the wrong way around.'

'No more secrets now. I guess you got it all worked out, Mom.'

I had. Almost. The air was clear, the air between us. The living room was full of light, the pure bright light of the equator; we could see everything in the space between us, the clean circulation of thought; nothing tight, nothing suffocating.

It was just after lunch, we were drinking our coffee. Susan had on a pale blue sun frock which tied at the shoulders; so pretty against her hair, I thought. And said, 'Very fetching, honey. In fact, you look a perfect picture. Where's your camera? How about a snap for Augustus?'

She got up to find it, leaving me to hold Helen who wriggled with plump damp happiness on my lap. I spoke into her seashell ear.

'You and I, honey, are going to have good times together. I may look a perfect fright, just an old, old witch, but I'm your granny and I love you.' I was thinking about Mother and Nicola together, the walks along the beach, the talking. Just a few more years, I begged, just time enough for this.

Sometimes the story I have just written about events from death to death seems to have nothing to do with Nicola. She was always so vague, so spectral, hardly real, whereas Susan was the one at the beginning and the end of it all. Did I do it for her? Was I always first and foremost her mother in all that occurred?

After Susan left I made myself busy. The roof needed mending, the woodwork repainting, and I decided to extend the verandah so that I might write outside to enjoy the early morning freshness – this work has only just started, I can hear them hammering now. I have also enlarged the vegetable patch so that we may enjoy a greater variety of produce, soil permitting

– 'we' being myself and Husseini's large family which has so cramped the servants' quarters that I will have to expand them – next year.

A month ago a vagrant artist came to me with Makonde paintings to sell. I refused his pictures – despite the usual story of infants dead from cholera – but commissioned him to paint Makonde animals on the side of the house. It has worked well; I am pleased with the parade of strange creatures that marches round the walls. I feel protected by them, magically, just as my pets in Njoro used to reassure me. I dare say one always needs reassurance of some sort, at whatever age.

Even more recently I discovered Mother's old fish tanks tucked away beneath the verandah. Perhaps Nicola stored them there. Collecting has become a passion with me. I find what I can at low tide, and send out Husseini's sons with jam jars to collect the lovely things off coral islands. Such colours, such variety: nature is endlessly inventive. Nonetheless I am always short of specimens. They never last long, you see. They die from wrong diet, fluctuations of temperature, or they fight, or mothers eat their offspring. But I do have one or two favourites who, despite all adversity, bravely insist on surviving.

You would be pleased, Mother.